d. s. smith

Falcon-Tor Press

Falcon-Tor Press
falcontorpress@gmail.com

Printed in the United States of America

ISBN - 978-0-692-98229-7

Second Edition

14 13 12 11 10 / 10 9 8 7 6 5 4 3 2

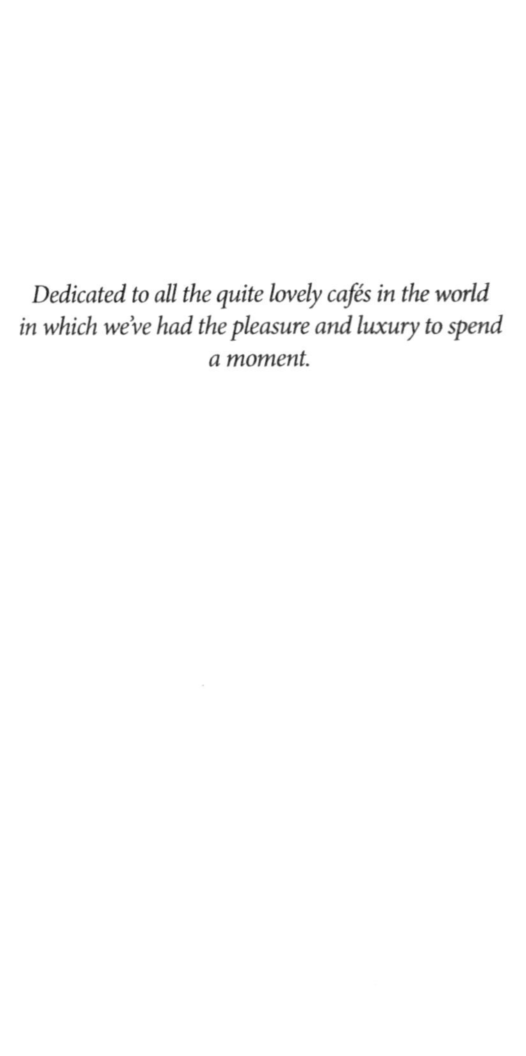

Dedicated to all the quite lovely cafés in the world in which we've had the pleasure and luxury to spend a moment.

1.

"Child, the grief pouring from him like sweat from a pig! Sucking, clutching, biting at it like a teat he can't get enough of. It's never been so good." Analinda's brown eyes grinned at the thought. William had come home from the forest yesterday morning after more than ten days at sea and cast his net upon her, pressed against the wall as the wooden floor creaked beneath their feet, forgetting in the moment that they had each floated out from shore on a raft of logs while Marginaul had been busy at work.

"What the fuck," you say? Well stick around and you shall see.

Throughout it all Marginaul worked. Day in and day out. Marginaul who lived with his quiet wife in three rooms at the end of the dusty road that formed a "T" with the square in front of the church was not a drowning man despite what others may have thought. Not the lifeless soul people spoke about. But then what did they know? Nothing more than what they saw. Nothing more than what they were told. A wife so quiet she was never to be heard from again. And it was better for Marginaul that way. To work undisturbed at his bench cutting cloth with a cat by his foot he named "Anjou." Awake or asleep, really the same. Its needs met, waiting only to be fed. Taking reduced to sport, the feline yawned and stretched her tail then skulked forward to make a play on a luckless fly, last seen hanging impaled upon her claw, it's still warm life a snack transferred quickly to the mouth. And still Marginaul worked. While outside a group of small children, maybe five but from the sound of their song probably not more than three, played in the road in the mid-afternoon sun. Not yet four, not yet time for tea, for those who could see the grainy dust sticking to the wetness of their skin lightening them to beige muting the contrast of their soles. And all the while Analinda and Maraqui began again.

"I think it scared him and now he's clutching, constantly grabbing at me." As the very soft, very dark, very warm Analinda went on, Maraqui smiled and replied "We all should be so harassed." "No, you don't understand."

Analinda said. Not haughty in her tone, no offense taken between old friends.

William hearing the women's voices, alerted to the presence of a visitor, composed him- self as he approached the stairs to come through the back door and into the kitchen. It was an easy enough task for him this day. He liked Maraqui. And his mind distracted for an instant imagining what it might be like, for an evening, or maybe more, the thought of her in pleasure, in a brief hug before he kissed his wife and came to his senses, he almost told her so.

And just as suddenly, it was as normally between them, William and Maraqui hiding from one another. A cordial exchange, a friendly "How have you been?", "Well, and you?", "No complaints", replacing any trace of intimacy. The two engaging in a dance they well understood. A game of tag they could carry on at length. It was appropriate. It permitted the three to remain friends while the women shared what William had learned to believe was thought and emotion.

"Maraqui saw '*Grey Matter*' last night." Analinda offered. "Really, how is it? I can't picture Goust playing the Turk. I see Johnnie C. in drag." William said speaking with a measure of animation.

"Yeah." Said Maraqui exhaling a snicker.

"But it worked, I liked it. He was surprisingly good."

To William's ear having heard it before it all sounded oh so educated and free, a bit above it all, as if they fancied themselves more aware than most - of the arts, of politics, of worldly affairs. And truth be told perhaps it were so, though still a man of the people William would not like it said. He took care to cover his tracks. This time like the last a plausible denial at the inquisition, believably detached. Anyway his words at an end, and the sound of his voice simply too inadequate to go on, for a fleeting instant, a genuine moment in time, William wondered if the contents of his stomach skittering across the kitchen floor might be criticism enough. Maybe something of substance to be found there if not above. But the queasiness suggesting that it might be so, was instantly overcome by self-doubt and a sense of clarity in the thought that the ladies might not be observant enough to see beyond the muck. And with the feeling passing as quickly as it had come, William suddenly found himself left with nothing but the certainty that Analinda and Maraqui were quite capable of going on with their conversation without him. Of course his ego being what it was, the man of the house so to speak, William felt compelled still to deposit his scent about the room. So raising his tail before excusing himself to go upstairs, he sprayed a subtle mixture of reluctance and haste. He wanted to leave the impression that he had something more pressing to do.

It was of course false. William spent his time pretending to busily occupy his time. Energetically producing nothing more than the illusion of being caught on his way to something more urgent. A game of solitaire played by one who was nearly certain that he had nothing of extraordinary value to impart to others except perhaps a degree of certainty about his lack of value, and the belief that maybe it caused him to be more enlightened than most. William affected a nonchalance about his gift which people seemed to find attractive in passing during a typical day. He was nice about it. Not pretentious in his way. A layer within a liar easily shed. He would readily admit the falsity of his act to almost anyone who might care to call him on his game. But of course there were so few who ever did that he usually found himself alone and uninterrupted, a past master in the contest that he had played since his youth.

2.

William had been brought to Veve as a child, his father having emigrated from the islands to the north after his wife and two older children had passed away. William the youngest and only surviving child of the pair had ties to Veve through his mother. Likeable enough, but somewhat solitary as a boy, slight of build and seemingly without special skills, William had been fairly easy to ignore. He had been treated with indifference by his father. His father, a man who in his generosity and openness had held his son at arm's length. A father who had had little time for a charge who reminded him of the pain he had come to Veve to leave behind. A father and son who seemed to grow to like it that way. William had often gone unnoticed for days at a time.

Always busy, never a moment to spare,

William's father threw himself into his work in their new home. So much so that William had difficulty remembering if he ever saw the man at ease. A man with an emotional range from arid to dry it seemed to William that father and son rarely, if ever, spoke. Communication without a word. Communication, to the extent that it may have occurred, by observation only. William grew to understand that between his father and him, tag was the game of choice in which the child was supposed to learn that "it" could never catch the wind. But still young, a child nonetheless, determined to play again and again until he might finally win, persistence his name before the change, for his effort, though uncertain through whose eyes to value the reward, William was eventually placed in a religious school where his talent was refined.

William looked back on those years through a haze. His vision impaired by time. His failing memory an anodyne for the pain. And despite the wisdom and disgust which he had acquired with age, he was certain that if given a chance to relive those early days they would remain unchanged. His contempt far too mild to fuel a rage to change the course of his journey. Too weak to have drawn his father near.

3.

The voices from below having stopped, the door having clicked to a close, William tucked in his shirt, straightening his trousers as Analinda's foot hit the last run of the stairs. Reaching the landing, she hesitated for a moment and caught her breath. As she entered the bedroom she scattered the rainbow of dust that fell through the skylight in the afternoon sun.

"Is Maraqui still here?" William said asking the obvious. "No, she had to go to work." "She doin' okay?" "Yeah, alright. How'd she seem?" "Like Maraqui." No great insight there. "What's she up to, anything? Anyone new?" "No, she just came by for a minute." Analinda put something on her dresser and turning back toward William, she asked "What are you doing home in the middle of the day?"

William, a gainful employee of the Government of Veve, worked in the office of touristic affairs writing copy for brochures and doing some of the graphics. Although nominally an eight thirty to five gig, like much of public work, there were certain perquisites if not overly abused. One of them was flexibility which fit William like a glove. It was a beautiful day and he had wanted to go home.

A self-deprecating but faintly sly grin passed across his lips. A twinkle flirted with his eye. William thought it might be fun to give it a try. So reaching back into his throat, he rooted about, certain that it was there to be found hidden down amongst the folds deep below the base of his tongue. He searched quickly, certain that he did not have much time. His wife was not a patient soul. But he was having trouble finding just the right sound for the machismo that he wanted to use and fumbling under the gun finally uttered "I've come for you, woman." The voice forced, a feeble baritone, it fell to the floor with a hollow thud. And William knew immediately, as soon as the words had escaped, that a call to casting would have to be made. The part had not required the cave man to show up with anemia and then trip over his club.

Analinda smiled, patted William softly on the chest, and then wedged her feet into a faded pair of espadrilles. "I'm going down to the studio, I'll be back in a while."

Analinda and William lived in a small house which they had managed to further reduce in size with their accumulated clutter. What was once a single-car garage stood across a swath of grass at an angle from the back door to the kitchen. Although at first not terribly handy, overtime William and Analinda had through trial and error become sufficiently skilled to convert the garage into a studio where Analinda made art and carved out a living.

Analinda created life. She was able to share with others forms conceived in her mind for pleasure. And not anxious about her time, for the moment she could offer herself the luxury of exploring her emotions and thoughts. She was happy.

The wind, really just the soft movement of hot air, pushed Analinda's moist clothing against her brown skin as she scuffed her way across the grass toward the studio. The next-door neighbor yelled at her small child, a swift circled overhead. The afternoon was like a hundred others on Veve. A summer's day in the tropics that would pass without a storm.

Left behind, upstairs, alone and unrelieved, his call to casting unanswered, William bowed to Onan before conducting ablution. A moment later taking stock, he realized the ceremony hadn't helped, but there was nothing more that he could do, at least for a while. Physiology being what it is.

4.

William ran down to the kitchen, grabbed some guineps and walked out the front door. As he moved with seeming purpose along the dusty road to town the thought that he might be discovered, gone, out of the house without a word, proudly occupied a corner of his mind, small as it was. Really little more than a square no longer able to be called a green, it marked the intersection of a vacant lot and an abandoned petrol station in a deserted postage stamp of a town. Opposite the small corner from where he stood William mulled the consequences of annoying his discoverer, the possibility of her wrath. He tried to linger a moment longer with his thoughts, but the signals at the junction were beyond his control. The traffic lights changing from red to green and green to red, it was time for his petty conceit to be on the move. But for a second it did not budge, it just stood there out of gear, until a horn blaring somewhere behind his eyes jolted him into motion, causing William to shift and get his vanity out of the way. And with his mind, for however briefly, functioning again, he realized that in all likelihood his absence would probably go unnoticed.

Beginning to enjoy the exercise, he picked up the pace of his walk. To his left far beyond the rooftops of the houses he could see the sea. On the uphill side of the road cement staircases cracked from age and the strength of wild grass climbed up to homes that would continue to be passed down to the generations to come. Homes which had been built to survive the monstrous hurricanes which arrived every two decades or so to cleanse the island and remind the people to be thankful for what was there. Storms which taught them not to take the island's beauty for granted.

As William descended into town he saw the "Ice House." A two story white clapboard structure in need of paint with an exterior balcony that faced the port. Hot and with no particular place to go it seemed a logical stop. It was doubtful that he would run into anyone who might care that he was not at work and it was a comfortable spot to kill some time. A place where people left each other alone unless invited.

William pulled open the screen door offered as a courtesy to the guests of the establishment, a bulwark against the flies and other pests attracted to human sweat, and walked into the darkened room. The slatted shutters pulled closed to limit the sun and reduce the heat inside. The Icehouse an ancient structure in its own right, owed its name to history and its original proprietor's sense of a commercial turn of phrase. It was built on a parcel of land where at the turn of the last century an icehouse stood before burning to the ground. In its present form, the Icehouse served cold drinks. As to the fire with all that water inside the insurance investigators did cast a dim eye but it is said that the limits were eventually paid and that with the moneys from the policy and the sale of the land the original owner moved to the main island and started a small business selling retail goods of some sort. Of course that was many years ago and the event is now just a part of the lore.

Standing still, listening for what he could not see, William waited for his eyes to adjust to the lack of light inside. The main room only gradually coming into focus, slowly revealing airplane propellers circling overhead as they gently fanned the air, while a few feet away, shoulder high, two flies silently held pattern stacked one above the other in triangular flight. At a card table in the far corner a woman and three men played dominoes.

During the day when the waitresses were still asleep or at least nowhere in sight, customers had to ask the barkeep standing behind a tooled mahogany affair with polished water stains for hard alcohol. It was serve yourself out of a cooler for soft drinks and beer.

The chill of the water and ice surprised William as he plunged his hand deep into the open chest. He fished about for a suitable drink and with bottle in hand staked out a table nearby but away from the others. He poured a draught of the cold liquid into the back of his mouth and then placing the bottle down on the table to reserve it for himself, he grabbed a cue from the opposite wall and set up a diamond for nine-ball.

As he shot a round he thought back on the history of this part of the city and the buildings like this one which had entertained the sons and daughters of Ile-Ife, Bakongo and Gao. The men and women who created the generally unpublicized family fortunes that governed his life. The Cristophes, McTurmans, Jeffersons and the like who through their cunning and greed had spotted a need and filled it.

To the extent that he knew the history, he understood them to have been crafts persons, traders and brigands who settled their differences and combined their skills. Overtime they moved their own as well as the nation's capital to the main island of T'Embour, the place which gave the country its name. And there they built the economy from which William, Analinda and others of their type fled after university. But Veve was their source, the place where they maintained vacation homes and burial sites.

These people whose spirit, for good or bad, defined the island. Serious and driven and wise beyond their years, and now quite fucking dead, though still controlling from beyond the grave. Their bony fingers holding their progeny by the shoulders. William imagined them alive, cocksure men and strong saucy women who knew what they wanted and grabbed it from the air. Living hard and fast and with a spirit that after all these years was still alive and couldn't be shaken by William and his kind who weak as they were maintained and admired what the founders had wrought.

William looked through the banister to the closed doors of the rooms on the second floor and conjured the din of a night long past when the future was being made. When the brothers and sisters one hundred years or more ago were busy shaping William's day. Who for a few moments gave into their youth and energy and allowed themselves to play. And the music was loud and it was hot. And the man strode the 88's and there was sweat in the air. And it was dark and William was there when one of them pulled his mother's mother close and grabbed her by the ass and rocked against her floral dress and spread her thighs. And William was there in the mouth of the man when he placed himself on his knees and held the soft bars of her gate in the palms of his hands and spoke in tongues begging for entry to her womb. And William was there and could smell the sweet scent of hyacinth too.

"Domino!" A man shouted from the corner. And William was here in the Icehouse empty except for a few persons on a lazy afternoon. A cue in his hand. And he stood for a moment gathering his bearings, then walked to his seat and sipping his drink, started to warm to the idea of being alone. A buzz gathered in his head as he finished the bottle. And ready to leave he placed the cue in the rack, and paid his tab and entered the street. And for an instant blinded by the light, eyes tearing, he couldn't see the path of gold lying on the surface of diamonds that shimmered before him.

5.

Down the road Marginaul pulled out his pocket watch. It was time to close. He turned over the rectangular cardboard sign, its block lettering stating the fact, locked the door and drew the shades. As the shop fell into darkness, Anjou sensing that her work day was also at an end showed a certain vigor. The cat put her rump in the air and extending her forepaws, stretched before letting out a yawn. Then, exchanging the sway of her back for an arch, she closed her mouth as her stretch transformed into a shudder, the tremor retreating along her spine and passing through her body to emerge from her tail like smoke from the tip of a flickering flame. Relaxed and again at ease she followed Marginaul into the living quarters behind the shop.

The home was spare, but not entirely neat.

It connected to the shop through a door that could easily be mistaken for a closet though once inside one found a home that was surprisingly light and airy. The main room, painted in a washed but vibrant yellow that was trimmed around the doors to the kitchen and bedrooms in a blue that was much darker than the wood planks that lined the floor, opened onto a screened porch that was set down a step and looked out onto the sea. An early evening breeze greeted the pair as they came in.

Marginaul turned on the console television set about which his infrequent visitors could be counted on to remark: "When you goin' get rid of that old thing" or words to that effect. But he had no intention of doing anything of the kind. When he bought it, the set had been an itch that he had scratched, an extravagance indulged by a frugal man. It worked still perfectly well and he saw no need to replace it.

The voice of a newscast accompanying him, Marginaul walked into the kitchen. He opened a can of food for Anjou and started dinner. At lunch he had gone down to the market and bought a kingfish steak to broil with curry, and onions, and pepper, and some plantain that he intended to fry with garlic and ginger, all to be eaten with yesterday's rice. Tasty guests that he knew would arrive on time.

Finishing his knife work, the marinades from the afternoon complete, he put the fish in the broiler and went to a cabinet to find a pot and pan to place on the stove. As he placed the moist soft fruit of the plantain into the pan, the clatter of a spume of hot oil fleeing the site momentarily shoved the voice of the newsperson from the kitchen. He lowered the heat and covered the pan, calming the plantain down.

Everything in order, the flames not too high, Marginaul felt that he could leave the food to cook on its own, at least for a while. So he walked back into the main room and sat in his padded reclining chair in front of the tube. But growing a bit nervous after a minute or two, the plantain needing to be flipped, the rice needing to be heated, he got up and returned to his place in front of the stove. Watching and waiting until when everything was done he drew a plate from the cabinet, drained the plantain of its excess oil, and pulling a fork and knife from a drawer grabbed a couple of bakes from a yellow tin to the right of the stove, then with all in order, he poured himself a tall glass of ginger beer, and on a portable tray made to latch in place and stand on its own served a dinner for one in the main room in front of the TV, in front of the pictures of the events of the day, where he could better hear what, if anything of interest, the voice had to say.

"A ship carrying refinery parts has run aground south of the outlying islands. A search and rescue team has been dispatched. The price of gasoline may be impacted modestly. Details and analysis not to follow.

A summit of the G-12 will be convened in the capital in early April of next year.

The mayor's youngest daughter has been bestowed the prestigious Windward award for excellence in math at the collegiate level.

And now for sports and a commercial break."

Marginaul looked to his plate for sustenance and was not disappointed. At the half hour he turned off the set, and went into the kitchen where he cleaned up his mess and brewed some coffee. He would pick up his reading as he did every evening from the spot where he had left off the night before.

6.

The idea of a bottle of wine, or more likely not willing to go that far a glass or two, aroused in Maraqui's mind a blood red dizzying embrace in a slip, makeup smeared, stumbling on pretty limbs beyond control, lost for days behind a locked door, floating, aware of the high, belly full and well, above the limits of her conscience to awake on the other side purged of her exhaustion with a lung emptying scream alleviating the pain that rested in her mind and body. She too who lived alone wanted to go home and swallow as much as she could take.

Maraqui had seen the movie late at night many times before. She who knew the lines word for word, but an understudy at heart, forever feeling unprepared. No scarf, dark glasses, or upturned collar on an overcoat, she was never quite able to get herself to stop at the store to consume the part. She who craved abandon could never let go long enough to pay the fare, let alone jump upon the transport.

But this time the city, or maybe it was the presence of the reflection of something alive within, interrupted her fear and she lost her balance. And turning back from where she'd come, she formed - no, pausing for a second not bold enough for such an act - joined a vicious mob in throwing stones at the quadriplegic she so despised when she passed this way. With each throw her voice growing louder and louder, shouting, screaming becoming one of the most vocal among them. Until finally growing weary, unable to raise her arm, confused and ready to implode, she stumbled forward only to break her fall in a kiss planted softly upon the cripple's cheek. And there resting her head against its shoulder, taking time to breathe, not even having to ask, it bade her to forgive what she had almost done. And who could resist when offered, that the moment would quickly lose its bite and soon recede? Not Maraqui, that was for sure. Thankful for such beneficence, she gathered herself now certain that her action warranted no more than a glimpse. And no longer much caring what the mob might think or that it might observe the disability so prominently on display, anesthetized and immune from its wrath, she returned to the crawl she had fully mastered long ago. And after selecting a few groceries as a camouflage, and in a nod to a concern about her health, she placed a bottle of Not Sterno in her cart and prepared for the show.

7.

"William." Analinda walked into the kitchen and stopped to wait for a response. Nothing. She yelled out again. "William." Still no response. Odd, she thought. She walked through the kitchen, stuck her head through the door to the den then hesitated before beginning the climb upstairs. "William?" A note of mild concern in her voice as she placed the ball of her right foot on the run of the first stair, and slowly, softly started the ascent alert for the hint of someone unexpected, watchful for a trace of anything red from a pool on the floor in one of the rooms above.

They rarely if ever locked the doors to their home. Life was still safe on Veve and she thought to herself how foolish and silly she could be. Still she knew that they were not immune from the troubles which they heard constantly plagued life abroad. She moved cautiously but with some athleticism forward onward up the stairs. As she approached the landing she called out again. "William." The lights on the second floor were off. The sun had set and what was left of dusk allowed her to cast her fears among the shadows on the darkened walls. She pushed open the door to the bathroom at the head of the stairs, and then to the bedrooms to either side. Neither poised nor ready for anything though she may have thought otherwise, in her best imitation of a trained investigator she jerked open the doors. Empty and empty again. There was nobody else at home. "Damn him." She cursed. Why didn't he say something, anything? Honey, I'm leaving, I'll be back."

As bad timing would have it he wasn't there and now she was pissed. Her shift in mood immediate. She went into the bathroom and peed and then quickly returned downstairs, her pace accelerated by the anger that now stepped all over the joy that she had carried from the studio into the house. She had wanted to share a moment in time with her husband discussing a piece of her work. She had wanted his opinion. A few minutes emotionally, intellectually together, in union. But he wasn't there.

Lately William had begun to display an

uncanny ability of not being around on the few occasions she really wanted to talk to him. In this respect things had changed over the years. Where once he had been the constant, indeed, the source of stability in the relationship, now he seemed to be the one without gravity, floating out into space and wandering about.

Analinda groused a bit more, chewing on her anger until the irritation was gone and the flavor of its bile had passed. It did not appear to take as long as she would have thought and soon she began to feel almost whole again. The healing begun, she noted that it had seemed to hurt less than the time before. The last time he had disappointed her.

Analinda was not patient with herself or others, and she was not forgiving. Not cold, just quick to decide and once decided, resolute. When the emotion was over she would say it was so and not relive it or care how she might be viewed. When she drew the line in the sand she would announce it once and it would be done.

With William she was not yet quite there. But it was coming and if it happened she expected that what they had been would end quietly and quickly. She did not see it getting nasty with fists, curses and shouting in the air. Not enough emotion left between the two. If it were so it might be different, might be nice, even fun, in the end. A damn sight more passionate than it had recently been. She'd be up for the fight. The taste of blood not unknown in her mouth. And if it went all the way and they didn't come back with vows renewed, she was certain that he'd be the one to be found and reported in the lurid press: "The lifeless corpse of a stranger in the back seat of a car slumped in a pool of urine and blood with nothing left from the self-inflicted wound but a stump where the face had been." The scarehead lead from the scratch and sniff news on Channel 164 with more to come at 10:00.

As the muscles in her calves propelled her stride Analinda conceded, and perhaps for the good, that she had not entirely shed her anger towards William after all.

The night air was sticky and hot, white curtains hanging outside open windows seeking relief from the heat. Men buried, possessed inside their mates unconscious, briefly lost, becoming conscious of being lost, diving in again only to find more air. So many moments that almost were.

Of late they argued over everything in meaningless spirals of emotion with no beginning remembered. A chase without peace or end. Every word, every action or inaction, intentionally misperceived in order to fuel the dispute. The past giving birth to a captious present and anger for a future fight.

William was not unaware of what was happening, the gulf between them not unknown. He knew early on of the coming of the tide and the separation of their souls. Of how they had come to stand on opposite sides of a wall by the edge of an ocean, able to see each other move but unable to touch or hear. A part of him had wanted to act immediately, to drive his hand across and through to the other side and grab her by the wrist and not let go, but he had hesitated, unsure of the risk, afraid that in making the stretch he might lose his balance and be swept out to sea. He had tried to remain hopeful that the water might recede on its own. And again and again he had kidded himself into believing it better to wait until, finally, it was too late. As the foundation beneath their feet slowly began to crumble, he saw her start to drift away.

And he wanted to scream and let his anger find form out of the mess that they had made. To let it take aim and spew forth in a shower of irrational words shouted to a hateful tune as if the shock from such crazed and ranting thought might scare her into making a change to the indifference that she showed him. But a direct attack not within him, preferring a more subtle approach he thought perhaps a homicidal ode set to a single chord played by a band so extraordinarily loud that the distortion would obliterate the grotesqueness of the lyric. Burying it in a tomb of sound so thick it could never be heard or attributed to him. And by the effort without effect, as he so often did, for his part he might feel purged with something ugly like this:

"Dear A,

I've been away. Or haven't you noticed, you bitch? You selfish frozen bitch. I want to choke the life out your disbelieving body. I want to stand astride your struggling carcass, my hands about your throat. The look in your eyes, the moments 'fore they close, see the certainty of my purpose, replace your repose. You fucking cunt! I want to rip out your soul with a latex glove, hold it, your conscious face above. If you don't know it by now, I hate you my love." Repeat refrain, go to bridge.

Dear A..."

8.

As William continued his journey, a slight buzz in his brain, he recalled with a smile how once he had cheated on Analinda with a woman he had met in a bar in a hotel on a short trip taken solely to get away, though he had said it was for business. How they had fallen into conversation and he had learned that the woman was there to visit the dying child of a recently deceased friend. As they talked over drinks the woman told William how the parent had gone before from a condition from which the child, a little girl, would soon follow. It seemed to William all quite tragic and torturously unfair, a parent dying a slow death, awaking each day, introduced a new, helpless to stop, the pervert that solemnly promises to fill the void when the parent is gone, a godparent to the innocent, there waiting to lead the child by the hand. And he thought of the little girl as she watched her future and past decay. And he thought of the woman and what she too must have been going through, though listening to her words he did not get the sense that she deeply or truly cared. A disconnect as she rattled off the facts, a suggestion of the inconvenience of it all.

She told William how the little girl had asked her to bring a picture of the dead parent to the hospital where the child now stayed, and that she had not had time to find one other than that which was then mimeographed and folded in her purse. Pulling it out, without the slightest trace of concern or reservation, she showed it to William, certain that it would be sufficient to fulfill the child's request and need. For his part, William thought the offering a bit off the mark, giving as a precious keepsake to the dying child the program from her parent's funeral, a mite callous. But who was he to say? And preferring not to criticize or, heaven forbid, offend, his distaste for the woman's insensitivity not sufficient to dull his lust, he opted to think that maybe the child was too young to read or know.

Soon after the conversation took a more positive turn. The woman growing more beautiful by the sip, they spoke of a number of trivial things. And finally convinced that she was truly a bit of a fool and, to boot, one with whom it seemed likely he would have some fun, his confidence no longer knew any bounds. So in a most friendly but assuredly professorial tone and as a counterpoint to the sadness of her mission in town he began to enlighten her on his philosophy of love and the insight he had come to know in the meaning of the phrase "to make love."

And so from the gentlemanly scholar to his gullible dear, wide eyed and not so innocent, the lecture began. "To the English speaking mind, the phrase 'to make love' may not be poetic in its sound, but it is deep and full in its meaning. On a very rare occasion we may meet someone with whom we 'fall in love,' but more often than not we enter into a relationship with another with whom we gradually 'become in love' as over time they become associated in our mind with pleasure. They give us pleasure and we grow to love them." He felt as if he were finding a stride, gaining momentum, starting to believe that what he was offering might sound not totally contrived. And much to his pleasure and surprise his prey appeared also to be listening.

"In its most concentrated sense that pleasure may be physical, sexual. And it is from repeated exposure to that pleasure that love grows. If one can allow oneself to receive pleasure from another frequently enough, he or she will grow to love the other. When two have sex they begin the process of creating love. They are 'making love' which over time and through repeated occurrence will cause them to become 'in love'. And their joy, they will from time to time share with others, if only through a smile, a passing nod, or a friendly hello. The world is a better place at such moments. Some people may make clocks, others cars, but my people 'make love.' And with a warm hint of sweet breath he brushed his lips along the skin of her cheek and whispered "welcome to this part of our country, I hope you enjoy your stay."

The woman moved closer, the message received, transmission acknowledged. And William, now sweet Willie, an imperfect instrument perfectly situated, the proprietor of an idea, smiled and mused to himself "Thy will shall be done." Clear about what was to happen next, following naturally as it did on the tail of what had come before, they stood and wove their way as quietly, straight and inconspicuously as they could to the elevator and selecting the number of the nearer of their two floors, moved up to her room.

In the morning of the day after the night, when the deed had been done, and done quite well, Willie remembered how he had admired the distention of his member worn and tired as he stretched before the mirror and peered lovingly at the reflection of it, himself and his captured doe. She sleeping quietly beneath a sheet. Walking about, shoulders back, disrobed, proudly displaying without inhibition his manhood limp before its exhausted prey. They had drunk, smoked, bathed, tasted one another balanced dizzyingly on the edge of consciousness. Seeking teeth and lips through the night, their teats bitten raw. Male, female aflame at the source. And with exquisite pain he had placed his sack in the palm of her hand, bowing down to the woman no longer quite the fool as previously thought and asking for forgiveness, bared his soul. And she who was more than willing to absolve him, when at that moment unable to hide, transparent to her, without motive or past, giving her trust she opened herself and against her belly, thighs spread wide, breast to breast, unposed, and spastic, accepted his confession, just for the fun of it.

9.

Maraqui threw back another glass of the tawny port and felt its warmth course across her breasts. Slightly drunk and giving into the dream. Heated blood plucking at her skin. She became intrigued by the thought of an imagined visitor running the pad of a forefinger along the inside of her thigh. She let her head slide, gently, into the soft crook of the thick arm of the burgundy couch and slowly raising the hem of her skirt, closed her eyes to await her guest.

Which without warning or grace exploded to life, piercing, nearly rending her heart with the violence of its percussive strike. Its electric pulse invading her body. Metal within metal suddenly shattering her space. And leaping to the call, she threw up her arms in front of her face before it could strike again.

Maraqui yanked the receiver from the cradle. Unsteady, she paused and tried to settle herself before offering "Hello?" It was uttered tentatively and slightly out of breath and masked what she really wanted to say, but suppressed. "Hello?" she repeated, somewhat more oriented and embarrassed than furious this time, but nothing came from the interruption at the other end of the line.

10.

Day 1:

Everything has suddenly changed for William in his dreamscape of conical hives made of granular dirt, apart, distinct, separate in its space. He places his feet on the ground and feels almost nothing. Only from memory does he know that the earth will hold firm. With each step a cloud of roiling particles depositing a fine layer of dust about his toes. It is as if his feet could push through to the space below, but they don't simply because of his good fortune. There is no sense of concern attached to this condition. A possible predicament unfathomed. Not astute enough to grasp the consequences, the notion of a continuum lost to his rich soles.

It has something to do with a trek about the Andes, or so it seems. Mountains, and aboriginal peoples, and peyote and similar agents of the spirit, his body as distant and inconsequential to his mind as a blade of grass. As weightless and distinct as any other thing. An object he can view but not touch. William has taken too much and is floating among the trees in the forest.

The lines on the bark, grooves, really channels, he thinks black, darker than the surface of the trees, darker than the backs of the brown ants within, padding towards what? Home? Food? With a stethoscope in hand, a rational mind descends, momentarily, to take control and draw a parallel to the sweep of jazz brushes on a snare.

In the village there is of course a kindred soul. No dream could be complete without one. His doppelganger, the lead amongst the chorus standing in relief against the cast. The anomaly of finding her (him?) worlds apart amongst the trees never enters his mind. She and her - brothers? To him, it's not clear. The three men with her, maybe a brother, but much older and two others, whom he suspects maybe cousins, but perhaps no relation at all. They walk towards him in silence returning he thinks from a funeral. The one whom he may have mistaken to be her brother - in a dark suit, a white shirt, black tie, a grey felt hat - leading the informal procession of four. His stride strong and brisk, effortless.

She, a few yards behind, keeping pace without motion while at a distance to her rear, the two others, almost walking together, follow. She is color and heat and the mistress of his mastery absolute.

Day 2:

On the second day of his visions William was less arcane and more in control of what he had consumed. He began to see things as they were, for what they had become, and for a time felt as if he were able to slip inside the object before his eyes. For a moment one again with Analinda as she stood before the window in the studio overlooking the sea drawing warmth from the mug of coffee which she held cupped in her hands.

Her lips put to the brim and feeling the steam play against her cheeks, trying to make herself stay up for the second night in a row with sweet cakes and espresso. An experiment in sleep deprivation and bad health. Sculpture as giving form to delirium. Her stomach upset and at the moment the clump of bile clinging to the back of her throat held more significance to her than the objects lying scattered about the floor.

Analinda picked up the hammer which she was using as a painter might a palette knife.

She repositioned a pair of goggles over her eyes and began once again to beat the pieces of glass held captive in the metal bucket. Green, brown, red, and blue fragments to be affixed to computerized skeletons covered in transparent plastic molded with clay pierced by nails dipped in wax and ultimately to be splattered with yellow paint symbolizing the post-millennial reconstruction of the family as the engine of reconciliation.

The project, as projects of this type so often tend to, was moving along swiftly, so swiftly in fact that she thought it might be completed soon except for the impediment being imposed by the yellow she wanted to use. She generally hated the color but this time couldn't get it out of her mind. She saw it tipping the pieces of clear glass like rubber to protect the curious fingers of little children, blind adults and domesticated animals. Her choices narrowed to four variants on a tone, she intended to decide soon enough she thought, and hoped, to avoid doing any serious damage to her body, or for that matter, soon enough to avoid raising the suggestion to herself or anyone else who might care to notice that a gift certificate for enrollment in a twelve step program of some sort might be appropriate. She was not about to spend a dysfunctional summer in search of the perfect yellow.

She brought the hammer down again into the too full bucket and churned the breaking glass, shattering it under the pressure of her hand. The shards noisily vying for her glove like a school of sharks at a bloody piece of meat. Standing straight up she held the bucket by its handle and with her right hand on its base threw its contents against the concrete wall. The splintered teeth falling on the rebound like phosphorescent dust from a magician's pail. Bits and pieces lying in a silent heap on a floor swept clear for the purpose. She carefully sorted through the fragments for scraps of art.

It had been a week since she had really thought about William, and much longer since she'd last heard a word that he'd said. Her time at home was spent in the studio, focused. She was in love with the concept of focus. All distractions erased, completely blotted from her mind. Her attention devoted only to her work. She reached for a triangular sliver of green and placed it against the spine of the figure that would be the mother of the family, and within reach of the father's hand. The children would be given a jagged metal spike.

Day 3:

On the third day of his dream Analinda confessed openly to him for the first time that she was never, in spirit at least, a participant in good standing of her family. Not that it had been a secret before, but she spoke openly of it and took the blame. Not admitting to anything bad, or wrong, but acknowledging a style that was off by a few degrees. The long and the short of it in increments of time was that she had a lot of trouble getting worked up about seeing anyone from her birth unit for more than a few minutes. The emotion and meddling and cuddling, the celebration that others in her group seemed so naturally to enjoy, she just could not share.

An anniversary of an aunt and uncle. An excessively lavish affair. An extravagant fuss for not even fifty years. Complaining about the expenditure of energy, money and good cheer, she forced herself to attend afraid of the noise her absence would make. Except for the several drinks, the presence of a cousin who seemed to hold the gathering in equal contempt, and the pleasure shown by the guests of honor at the end, she thought the whole thing unnecessary, a waste.

With anecdote in mind Analinda searched the studio for a spike, a large drive screw, to be placed with a hammer in a single blow through the forehead of the father. The intent of the artist who knew family so well, to relieve the effects of an anesthesia she believed to be generally about, in the air, in the sea. Interactive, the eyes of the father suddenly stretched wide, open, alive, the mouth engaging in a smile not hostile but in recognition of an old friend, the expression to be held for a full three seconds before the effects of the anesthesia set in again, and the hammer to be left for the next in line.

As Analinda worked the concept through she found honest the mother's lack of immediate reaction to the blow to the father's head. The woman, short but of sturdy frame reflecting her experience of successful childbearing, looked on objectively her expression unchanged. It would not be until she thought of the children that the couple had shared that she would become the grieving widow. And her children, their children, the kids, far from being oblivious to the scene, found the sheer force of the blow, the act of jamming a piece of metal through a skull, even their father's, horrifying.

The boy was eight, the oldest child, two years older than his sister. He had not been especially close to his father and of course would no longer have the opportunity to become so.

With the marriage over it would now be just his sister, mother and him. He was still very young and genuinely loved them. Analinda wanted to make it clear that he had much to learn. The innocence of his expression intended to tell the tale.

The little girl, petite, pixy, very intelligent. Her reaction would be much swifter, less subtle causing Analinda to draw back for a moment and ponder the insurance implications of a spike in the mechanized hand of a little girl poised for and capable of counterattack.

Analinda recalled the story of a child's body found mutilated by the side of the road outside the hill town of Wyntonship near where she lived. A story told to her as a girl by some older boys who wanted her to be their friend. At least on the day they told her the sadistic tale. Boys seeking to be young men trying to impress her with their imperviousness to her fears. She remembered being revolted and scared and having refused their offer to take her to the scene of the crime. Even then she had thought it a stupid assertion of power.

Her thoughts, the darkness outside, the sense of being on display in the lighted studio, made her uneasy. There was a slight breeze and the surf could be heard, but beyond this the night was silent. It was late, or early, depending on one's point of view. Most everyone was asleep. The music from the bars and the clubs had stopped hours ago. And the taxi drivers, that servant class so vital to the island's economy, had gone home for the night. To their homes in the hills with the swimming pools and marble tile which they paid for in cash.

Day 4:

Analinda imagined what it might be like to witness the type of violence documented weekly in the tabloids. Cringe inducing, eye averting, gut heaving carnage. The kind that sells like a slice of hot oily pizza covered with much too much cheese melted over a base of thick red tomato sauce in New York City on a sunny lazy summer afternoon. To be the uninjured survivor of a plane crash. To hear the wild, panicked dialogue of the near dead. To view the instant when frenzy gives way to stillness. To disengage herself from the wreckage, to look about. To attempt to comprehend, the present and her future.

A lone survivor. The subject of whispered innuendo, never fully believed, complicit. "You know there was someone else alive on that plane. She must've panicked and run, got out and didn't look back. I mean you can almost understand, the shock and all, but still she could've helped. Imagine the cries, the dying, crushed, belted in their seats amidst the flames, the twisted metal. She says there was no one left, all dead, you know she didn't check."

And then to walk about unscathed from such horror, quite unacceptable. A disfigurement of some sort required, even an emotional scar might suffice, but there would have to be a wound, some trace to elicit sympathy from the viewing public. Something to enhance, maintain, or heaven forbid, rehabilitate the image of our survivor. A disfigurement not so grotesque as to repel, but deep enough to underscore the patrician within. The underlying strength of character, the ability and willingness to carry on amidst the stench of the dead surrounding her. A mark so that far from placing blame at the feet of our survivor, the public would praise her. A sensitive soul caught at a horrific event spared death only by the will of the gods.

William thought it a silly dream for Analinda to have lost herself in but noted that perhaps it filled a need. Years ago as a student she had procured from the university store an aquiline beak which she affixed to her face during class and had since come to wear always. He noticed now that it seemed to have grown more prominent under the gravity of the event, the moments immediately before and after the crash so tragic, but in the end the nose could no longer sustain itself. The weight of its tip snapping her from her reverie.

Night becoming light. It would soon be dawn. Analinda was reaching an edge. Dirt crumbling beneath her feet. Falling free, and clear from the ledge. She started mixing colors. Wiping paint from hands to clothes and by accident to face and hair, lack of food and sleep beginning to take its toll. She reached to turn on the radio in the corner by the mattress where she sometimes slept, but it was not what she wanted, not what she needed. Three hundred years of assorted forms of music, unsolicited offers of advice, small gangs preying on tourists, large gangs preying on the rest, knives, guns and family tales could not stop her from spinning dizzily toward the seat of her pants. Confident of her privacy, she put her head down and succumbed to sleep.

Day 5:

The rain came. A cylinder of fog, grey mist in the distance, moving relentlessly forward, oppressing the earth beneath its path. A drop slams against a window left thoughtlessly in its way, for a moment clinging to the spot where it hits, its body deformed flattened on impact, it slides to the ground. The onslaught begun. A barrage against the dry earth. Broad green leaves springing to defend.

The wind rushed through the studio carrying water over the sill, and the smell of the storm, to Analinda. Lying face up, right leg bent, ankle behind the knee of an extended left leg, a figure four below the torso covered in a mottled T-shirt. Left arm parallel, running the length of her body, palm down, arched fingertips hanging from the side of a mattress, pointing to the floor. Right hand raised above her head, palm open like a pupil seeking the attention of a teacher. She lies oblivious to the sound of the section of crumpled newspaper flecked with red and yellow as it rustles against the wall in the corner opposite the window where the wind blows in treble.

The house, the studio and the land on which they stand came from her father and grandfather. Industrious, hardworking, members of the community now survived only by Analinda, a still childless artist, and her husband. There had once been a son and an older daughter, but no more.

When Analinda was twelve, her brother then eighteen, the young man of the family, died. He and two friends in a small boat, lost. The details were never clear. The boys hadn't told anyone where they were going and it wasn't known when they left. By the time anyone had reason to be concerned it was much too late. The search revealed nothing and for several years after, Analinda's mother maintained his room as he had left it. Ultimately, the family grew to hope that he was making a successful life elsewhere, having chosen to abandon them.

The loss of the sister was different, gradual. The decline visible. The end witnessed by all who cared to see it. A beautiful woman, strong, bright, buxom, given to color, laughter, and flirtation, that one day was no more. The energy drained from her life force creating a dowry of property and solitude for the youngest child.

The storm battered against the shutters of the studio and Analinda stirred. Tired, slightly ill, and hungry with a bad taste in her mouth, she rolled onto her forearms and knees, and cupping her head in her hands, groaned. She breathed deeply, finally mustering enough strength to stand, and making her way to the house, stumbled out of her clothes and into the shower, bare feet against the cool white tile.

Day 6:

By the sixth day the images, disconnected as they were, were coming fast. The multilayered photos of a spouse taken through a hole drilled in a bathroom wall by a husband betrayed. The lens increasingly distorted by an incensed mind which, despite the pain inflicted by the viewing of her crimes, was determined to capture it all on film, documented for the confrontation. The undeniable proof of her affairs. But it was a thought without a plan. A reflection from a man not quite sure of what he might do. Seated and tied to a chair with a gag in her mouth as he let the film role? "Action!" To be his shout. Perhaps, but doubtful, not the violent type, so able to contain his rage it might all go down without a fight. Though as he pondered the options he could not be sure. Not a lot in the way of money to be gained, and as for moral superiority, well, it just did not seem to have much of a bite. And so growing increasingly confused, not certain which way to turn, frightened that he might not get upset at all, terrified to possess such self-control, he tried to calm himself, softly, soothingly whispering "let it go, let the feeling go." And the winds quieted.

Day 7:

The brief storm having passed, the pleasure craft bobbed playfully on the surface of the water alongside the quay, and the tourists resumed their stroll among the downtown shops in the midday sun. The buildings, originally warehouses, converted to their present uses, providing shelter for the wholesale trafficking and discount retailing of the precious stones, clothing, and other wares that drew the offshore merchants and day-trippers to the Mart. Commerce awash in pastel under the blazing sun.

At a cafe just east of the main boulevard cruise ship passengers reflected on the relative costs of merchandise and their experiences at other ports of call while the proprietor mopped the floors around the several entryways that opened wide to the street. The doors, an effort to provide light and air into a brick room of walls lined to the ceiling twelve feet high by books and art. The cafe standing opposite the green where the high school band would practice later in the day under the shade of the gazebo dedicated to the memory of Aldophus Murphy. A local hero of inspirational mien, who served now as an oft bespattered perch. By the age of seven the school children having memorized his name and his contribution to the installation of the regime. Aldophus, Aldophus who led a cell of laborers through the fortnight of the siege.

Aldophus who gave of himself so that in a far corner of the cafe at a table removed from the din of tourists ignorant of the local customs teenage boys and girls could speak liltingly of the objects of their lust and the issues of the day. No longer shackled by a fear of consequences imagined, or paralyzed by their elders, boys much bolder than before and girls quite aware of the power of their charms, speaking unabashedly.

But still there was an innocence about them. Kids willing to listen to a performance of the high school band, members of the junior fellowship. Cynicism not yet a cancer on their soul, they smiled easily and believed they would always be happy. And when the appointed hour arrived they obediently returned to their homes for food and commune.

Day 8:

Marginaul sang to himself as he shuffled to the door to open the shop and begin the day. "Ilekun aanu Olorun, K'o si fun gbogbo wa; K'arun ma ba wa pejo. K'awa ma toroje. God's door of mercy, May it open to all of us; May no illness assail us; May we never beg our bread." A personal anthem. A part of a morning ritual, the singing of praises to Olodumare and the seeking of blessings for his shop.

And behold no sooner had he flipped the rectangular block lettered sign to read "OPEN" than a light skinned woman in a straw hat appeared at his door. A woman of middle age with fleshy arms, and pleasant enough manner, wishing to inquire of his services. A collector with a granddaughter who though ignorant of his craft had heard much about his skills.

"Good morning, sir." Said the woman. "It is. A beautiful morning, madam. What can I do for you today?" Marginaul replied. The woman, excited, a bit flushed, perspiring from the effort of climbing the hill to the shop said, "I have heard so much about your work, I can't tell you how thrilled I am to be here, and finally see your workshop and to meet you." A suppressed barely audible titter accompanying the slightly embarrassed confession.

"My husband insisted on taking a cruise. I hate boats, but it's been a dream of his, so of course I had to agree to go. But I made damn sure that if he were going stick me on a ship somewhere in the middle of the ocean that the boat would stop in Veve. This place is so beautiful, I can't believe I'm here." The woman momentarily catching her breath, placed the tips of the thumb, index and middle fingers of her left hand together against her temporarily stilled lips and gazed in wonderment about the shop at the detail of the work, the delicacy of the features, the intricacy of the carving. "I have a granddaughter. She'll be eight in July. I want you to carve her a doll house.... Please?"

Marginaul paused briefly to assess the woman and her request. He had more than enough work to meet his needs and it was not unusual for him to decline. Now that he was in semi-retirement he rarely undertook more than a few large pieces per year and those usually only for old friends or second and third generation clients. But he liked the woman's smile and to her relief he responded, "I'd be happy to."

The two discussed the details of a dollhouse seven rooms in all and the nature of the family to occupy it. His hands still steady despite the many years, Marginaul quickly, expertly drew a preliminary sketch capturing the ideas that he would later bring to life in wood. The logistics of shipping and payment resolved, the means for further communication addressed and after an hour, maybe two or three minutes more, the woman secure in the knowledge that her granddaughter's childhood would be changed forever, certain that it was for the best, understood that it was time for her to go. Unfortunately, however, no sooner had she stepped outside than her certitude was swept away.

As the tale has been told the plump and happy grandmother left the shop, but instead of immediately walking back down the hill and returning to the place from which she had come, she stooped to pick up something she saw blowing in the wind by the curb in the dirt opposite Marginaul's door. A mendicant's card, an almsgiver's muddied receipt inscribed with the words, "The spirits abound. They're all around us, touching our skin, playing tricks to confound us." Some have called the thing in the dirt a snare left to capture certain game, bait intended to attract quarry to a trap set by the dreamer, but that is probably not true since it seems the dreamer turned out to be the prey.

Anyhow, as she read the words and puzzled the thought, wondering how it might apply, it is said that a body scurried by her ankles. Four legged and furry, a panicked rat running for shelter on the opposite side of the street. But a little too late in grasping its predicament, not swift enough to escape, the animal was swept off its feet. A torrent of water, a wave from the sea, spinning its body, flipping its paws, forcing its head beneath the surface, away from the air, its tail a buoy marking its imminent demise.

Still as God is merciful the rat was granted a pardon, though unfortunately brief. Pulled from the flood limp but not yet drowned, its reprieve was short-lived, its neck accidently pierced by its savior, or so it is told; though to the grandmother who witnessed the event it looked more advertent than not. And if that were not enough for the poor old woman, sufficient to give her a scare, the rat's carcass now newly dead was next seen splashing in the water in the jaws of a fox. Water the color of red as thc rat's blood swirled in the wash about her feet.

All the while that this had been going on, in the seconds when the old girl's attention had been focused on the sudden shift from life to death, the fox's mate, yes, they traveled as a pair, had not been at rest. Ever alert, the mate, it is believed that it was a she, is said to have noticed the dreamer standing by the side of the road. And so with all eyes concentrating on the action elsewhere in the raging stream she began to wade quickly but without a sound through the water in search of this bigger game. Mind you, it has never been explained why she chose the dreamer over the grandmother, perhaps she thought him the slighter of the two, though it proved to be a strategic mistake.

A fight ensued which was vicious but quick, won by the dreamer, who agile and strong, was able to ward off the fox before its mate could join the fray. Having bought a moment or two and maybe a bit more, but knowing that he could not stay, it is said that the dreamer ran to conceal himself in the nearest room. The room in truth was really nothing more than a closet, though fortuitously one which offered a second door as a way out. As the dreamer sprinted through the first door with the foxes on his tail he slammed it behind him, the crisp closing accomplished with all his might, it greeted him with a pleasant hello. His ear happy to hear one of the foxes scream in pain, its paw, all that had made it across the jamb, crushed and severed by the blow.

Now feeling safe even though the room was dark, ensconced with limbs intact, the dreamer had time to relax, or so he wrongly thought. He drew a breath and started to sigh, but his relief soon left him, not even half uttered before it turned to dismay. Because finally adjusting to the lack of light, his eyes could plainly see that there by the other door was a leopard seated comfortably on its haunches drumming its claws and about to bare its teeth.

As for the old lady, the loving grandparent of the tale, it is said that with the water miraculously withdrawn she immediately returned the card to the ground, respectfully replacing it as near as she could recall to the spot from which she had removed it. And then in an extended request, an offering intended to invoke the beneficence of whatever might be listening, she prayed for the health of her family.

Day 9:

By the ninth day William was no longer well. He was thinking how he might go about it. Killing two birds with one stone so to speak. A fist pounding at a door to be timidly opened by a woman who finds standing before her, a friend of a friend. A male, obviously confused, desperate, and disoriented having chosen this door and this woman who is single and alone. But they know each other, this man and this woman who could be friends, but for the spouse of the other. And he desiring to love her, wanting to love her, to spite the other. His head bowed trying to convey his need, vulnerable but certain in his doubt, still his passion faked, the dishonesty shining through, she will not be fooled. Knowing as she does that he has turned to her because she seems alone, disconnected from all but one in his world. No corroborative witnesses to the lust that has brought him there to lay his head upon her slip white against her bosom, for the comfort of her arms.

And the woman shares the deceit, it having been far too long. And without a word she responds pulling him to her body, softly floral, oiled, pleasing. And he breathes deeply of her scent, awakening a spot long dormant at the back and base of his brain, a light, a source of energy, guiding his cheek across her breast, his palm along its curve.

William thought of Maraqui in these terms. To run his hand along the swell of her belly, to rub her fur, to bring her to a head. To possess her, both her and his wife. But he was not man enough, not yet. Still suffering as he did at the sudden sight of a beautiful woman in the street. A stranger appearing at a moment not yet prepared for her. How he would have liked to have been able to approach such a person simply (no, simply maybe a lie) to tell her of the effect. Her face, her eyes, the movement of her body beneath her clothes, what it did to him. But of course convention prevented such honesty and the conflict hurt his head.

Poor William. It was at moments such as this that he might actually have found himself at Maraqui's door. Attempting to establish what he knew not to be the truth. A semblance of control over his life, still a free man. But he couldn't do it. Forever laughing at the triviality of such a demonstration, trying to think more deeply about an act appropriate to prove his worth, to himself and to the other. But always his concentration lasting only for a minute, out of self-conceit, distraction, and delusion, and with the comforting knowledge that he would cross this ground again, for want of greater strength destined to trudge over and over up this very hillock, he would dub himself the son of Aeolus, though modestly acknowledging that he lacked the guile of the former's the past.

Day 10:

He would subsequently admit under questioning to not being wholly discomforted by the notion that his daily log might be mistaken for the memoir of a pervert. Ten days out from shore and still William could not get the picture to leave his mind. The tip of his forefinger smoothing the coat above her mons, stroking, arousing, engorging the vestigial male within. Her legs, her thighs. Kissing, soothing her worried brow. Maraqui the vulnerable. Maraqui who would give herself to him for the pleasure finally given to her. It could be. He knew it could be. But he stopped himself aware that all the others have said the same. The infatuated, the deluded, the stalkers, the pedophiles, they've all known it could be. William the Different, William the Duke of Lust? Perhaps, but what if she said, "No!"?

Pausing, William began to think that there might just be a place for the spoken word before the deed. A bit of caution before the trial and sentencing. "I didn't mean it. Please,

please, give me another chance, give me a break!" Crying, kicking, screaming, clutching the leg of the defense table as the bailiffs carried him back to lock-up. "My God man it's only sex, please don't do this to me, I'm sorry!" The sound of his pitiable voice fading in the distance, suddenly cut-off by the slam of the solid metal door.

A serious case of the horns, like everything else, not to be taken seriously. A man with a beautiful wife who wouldn't give it up. "An artist, ain't she supposed to be a freak? What's happened? All that weird ass sculpture. Her arms up to her elbows in clay." William envisioned Analinda in the shower rubbing her body clean. Hot, water streaming from her shoulders, down her back, between the cheeks of her ass, along her legs, running off her teats, dripping from her pubic hair, hanging, soapy, heavy, soaking wet. There was a time when they shared bed and bath. When she was, a freak! But now it's no more than that, with nothing there between the two.

From a window, a radio, a voice, a newscast penetrated his mind, driving his thoughts away. "For the sixth day in a row the western sector has been the scene of unrest as minority investors have taken profits following reports of better than expected employment figures. Trading curbs continue in place. An investigation will be undertaken on behalf of the majority." The same noise, the same palliative blather. He wondered briefly how long the radio had been on, insinuating itself into his head, creeping towards critical mass, interrupting, but not for long, the images in his mind.

Day 11:

A double bed, a yellow coverlet, the color of the sun in a child's crayoned drawing, pulled back to reveal a plain white sheet against a brown form, attached to hair, tufted, and jet-black. It is morning in a small white room. An austere scene from a faraway countryside, a print framed on the wall. A mirror by the dresser. A corner room with three windows, opened from the sill, the one at a right angle to the other two, paint cracking from age, the interior protected from the annoyance of flies, mosquitoes, beetles, hemipterous insects and the like, by screens, still serviceable, though rusted and bowed.

When alone? When no one is watching? Does she touch herself and where? Do her muscles tense and quiver? Does she stretch and twitch? Generally not possessed of laudable thoughts, William, a simple man wanting to fuck for the sake of fucking, has noticed as he has grown older, perhaps a little wiser, that it has become more enjoyable. No longer able to look upon them, at least those of his own age, in the same way as before. With each crease, a bit of character, a bit of strength, more judgmental, of freer will, more certain in their way. The mind and body coalescing in a hole. Not entirely off-putting, he concedes. Elements emerging, a purer stone, with fewer fears on which to play.

He wondered if he could really just march over there and talk. Admit his thoughts. They'd known each other, though not well, for years. The husband and the friend acquainted through the common bond, Analinda, the spouse at odds with her mate. The "best" friend, a synonym for "truest" as in truth, as in "I want to, but I can't, please, please don't make me"? Or as in "I don't want to, I won't, and this will be told"? The latter a total loss, nothing gained except a complete and detailed report promptly forthcoming to a spouse.

But wait, ever the optimist, William, able to dismiss the clouds as if they were not there, capable of finding a ray of sunshine no matter how slight, it all suddenly seemed so clear. Well, let's just say he was hopeful. Perhaps they might choose to punish him for the vileness of his betrayal. A wife and friend, sisters as it were, sullied by the wantonness of such a contemptible disease ridden flea. The mangy weasel to be visited and interrogated by the Gestapo. Officers in jackboots with black leather masks, cat-o'-nine-tails and tumid garters barking orders that he would have to obey. "Down on all fours, you sweaty little rutting pig!"

Convinced it was worth a try, William rooted about for a directory, found a telephone and dialed. The ringing on the other end interrupted by the sound of a woman's voice, "Hello". "Maraqui, it's..." "... I'm not in right now but if you'd like to...." William hung up, both pissed and relieved, fate having answered his question for now. Still, stubborn, certain to try again, eager to have his nose put to shit like an undisciplined mutt. A trainee in his land of surreal dreams where the victims of rape step forward into the light transformed into happy souls. Where willing participants divorced from reality, and the bodies involved, experienced an opiate induced orgasm as never before.

Day 12:

In his fantasy, the object of his stroke, he saw her in a blouse open to the fourth button whispering to the pleasures within, the soft flesh inside. In pants, no, a skirt above a muscled thigh, she is lean, born elsewhere, an outsider to Veve. Maraqui was of the island through family visited on occasion as a child, but until recently and a brief stint while in school she had lived always abroad. But for some reason she had lighted here, a place she seemed intent on calling home. Perhaps the attraction lay somewhere hidden within Analinda with whom she had shared a room in her final undergraduate year as an anthropology student on semester exchange at the University on the main island. The two having managed to maintain their friendship ever since. At first via letters from overseas and now in person, in the flesh.

William found it curious that Maraqui seemed to be finding a home in Wyntonship. Not that Wyntonship was such a bad place, mind you. As a port of destination for those who wished to live in comfort and ease it was simply perfect. But as to Maraqui it would not have seemed quite such a snug fit. Itinerant by nature as the story was told to him, and after all she had supposedly done and seen, he might have thought she would stop to catch her breath and then be on her way. But instead she seemed to be making a home of the place. Word was that she had fueled her travel by working occasionally to supplement a meager inheritance. But he could not recall hearing of her staying for any extended period in a place as comfortably bourgeois as Wyntonship on the island of Veve. Maybe she had run out of money. He didn't know.

"Maraqui's here, Maraqui's there." Long letters in envelopes with colorful stamps, aerograms with minuscule writing arriving sporadically to tell a tale of a moment in time in the life of a foreigner at home in Doundouru, of a festival for Iemanja, of a Buddhist monk in flames. And after an expression of envy to each such scribe, the more settled of the pair, Analinda, would pen a story of her own.

Maraqui did not speak much about the stresses of her travels. An attractive woman, alone, young, without a home, it could not have been easy. Moving by train or bus, arriving somewhere, perhaps to find an acquaintance to be taken on for protection and good cheer, before a kiss good-bye and departing, the cycle repeated again, and again. Over time the comfort described by Analinda in her own letters apparently won out. One day a letter arrived from the United States announcing a need to rest and Maraqui soon followed.

She stayed a few days with Analinda and William, then moved on, to a one-bedroom house. And before long she had landed a job in a small boutique downtown in the Mart. That was almost two years ago. Yet despite the layer of stability, William was not convinced that her life had changed all that much.

The hip, the artists, and appendages thereto, comprised a permanent community in Wyntonship, very visible though not large in number. Eventually, through someone, everyone within the group, knew everyone else, even if not well. Since Maraqui knew Analinda, and so was seen about in proper company, welcoming parties were dispatched to greet her shortly after her arrival. But Maraqui refused the invitations to join and schmooze seeming to prefer to be alone, spending time on the beach, reading, apart from her surroundings, guarded, as if ready to flee on a moment's notice. Immune to the needs of the community, she resisted the advances with a sadness and weariness behind her brown eyes that pulled rather than repelled. Her refusals were misunderstood. People would come to her anyway, deep in the belief that they could succeed where others had failed, searching for vicarious thrills and a reward for relieving her pain. And all concerned, the married, the unmarried, male and female, found Maraqui, the foreigner, compelling, faintly resembling themselves, quietly full of secrets from a life unknown. There almost seemed to have been genuine affection toward her within the circle, if its members had been capable of that.

Perhaps Maraqui promoted the push and pull. Drawing a cloak about herself, not giving very much away. In conversation she was not snobbish. It was more wary. When approached, she was friendly, but brief, as if in a hurry. Looking at her react to others William thought she gave the impression of responding like a healthily anxious person. Her lack of enthusiasm an attempt to avoid lingering too long in the presence of charming phlebotomists. But as sensitive and aware of the situation as he was, even with him she would not open up.

Except once, not long before his call, at a party given by a gallery owner on vacation in Veve. The sun setting against the masts of the boats in the harbor. The wine flowed, the champagne spuming from the lips of the bottles, for a brief instant Maraqui seemed at ease. She spoke to him about a sunset far away in time and place and of a woman who had taken her in at a moment when she had been lost. She told him how it had puzzled her that the woman seemed to expect nothing in return. And how she had stayed a few days and wanted to stay more but couldn't because she didn't know how to further accept the woman's kindness without pay. And so rather than letting her unease destroy what the woman had done, she thanked her and ran away from her home.

Maraqui didn't relate the story to anything other than the sunset. She didn't describe the woman, she didn't explain where she went afterwards, or in what way she had been lost. The story came out in a moment disconnected from context and time and it passed out of existence as soon as she had uttered it.

Day 13:

All in all Maraqui appeared to have adapted well to her new scheduled and sedentary life, full of unremarkable days. The house in which she lived was ordinary but nice, not at all dark. An open place where one might expect friends to drop by. Maraqui planted flowers, red, white, purple, and pink, along the brick walk that led from the street down to the front door. On a morning or two one might even have caught her on her hands and knees in shorts with gloves weeding the garden. In the back she cleared a private area for sitting, reading, or hanging clothes to dry. And when she was at home, which was often, the windows and doors would be left open spread wide, music wafting softly in the air.

On its face it hardly seemed the site of the unnatural acts William wished it to be. Her neighbors saw Maraqui as quiet and gentle.

They had no reason to think otherwise. She was friendly in her greetings when she saw them. All was very normal, except to William who quite to the contrary was convinced that the house and its occupant possessed an inner room, a basement, somewhere closed from view, a place where the little lady of unusual bent came out to play.

Intent to find the chamber which he was certain was there, William resolved to one day burglarize her home. Adorned in black leather dress stealthily running his hands through drawers of satin underwear probing for a secret door, a button, a diary, in which her secrets would be revealed, confirming to him what he had known all along. But William knew he was not entirely safe in his pursuit, so determined to unmask the truth. To see for himself, to reach out and touch the padded walls, black and red. To see the instruments of pain, the grainy photos of Maraqui with dildos, whips and chains. All this whirling about his head as he touched himself.

"She was a nice girl. Never bothered nobody." To hear it told by the wrinkled old lady on the six o'clock news. Normally wizened and toothless, she had been told they were coming and spruced herself up in a patterned frock and before the camera spitting past false teeth, capitalized on her moment of fame.

Making the story up on the fly as the body bags one-by-one passed behind her and out through the lens. "Who would've known?" Well, William for one. Feeling his tongue on the inside of her thigh, the smell of her sex, warm and moist in his nose. He knew the truth from day one. The truth about sweet, gentle Maraqui, the quiet woman who lived on the other side of the door.

11.

"Dangerous" would not have been a word that would have leaped into his mind if he were asked to describe himself William thought. He couldn't see himself knowingly dispensing pain. But he was no longer so sure about "obsessive." He could feel it gnawing away little by little, nibbling at the routine of his life like a fluke in his belly, wanting more.

12.

"Hi. How are you?" It was Analinda calling on the phone. "Okay, what's going on?" Maraqui responded. "The same, can you talk?" Asked Analinda. "I have to be at work at noon but other than that I'm free." Said Maraqui. "Do you want to get some breakfast?" Asked Analinda. "Sure, where?" Answered Maraqui. "Suba's?" Analinda suggested. "Great, ten okay?" Said Maraqui. "Yeah, meet you there."

Maraqui finished dressing and threw a towel over her shoulders before drawing her hair back into a plait. Holding a mirror awkwardly behind her she inspected the reflection of the single braid in the mirror on the white wall in front of her in the bathroom. She patted the braid neatly into place with her left hand and satisfied, put the mirror to rest next to the sink, hung the towel on a brass hook held by three screws in the back of the door, and turning on the faucet rinsed a few loose strands of hair down the drain. On her way out of the bathroom she stopped at the spot where she had earlier stepped out of her grey pajamas, now cool to her touch, having transferred her heat to the wooden floor. Picking them up, she carried them to the bedroom and tossed them casually onto a couch cluttered with magazines.

She made up her bed, took a last look in the mirror standing in the corner by the bureau near the window and then walked through the living room to the kitchen where she poured herself a glass of orange juice. Sitting on the bench by the table against the wall as she drank. The sunlight falling through the window above the sink opposite. The cold glass in her hands. She stared at the bits of pulp on the surface of the liquid, floating, thinking about absolutely nothing, enjoying the taste. Then tilting her head back, she let the last bit of juice stream from the cylinder, the rush in and about her mouth caught with the palm of her hand. A final bit of housekeeping before leaving, rinsing the glass clean in warm water from the tap, she turned it upside down on the drain board to dry, ready for when she would return. Moving back through the house, through the living room, past the couch, she picked up her bag from the table by the front door, pulled it to a close behind her, checked the lock, and began the five minute walk to the stop where she would wait for the bus.

Suba's was a noisy crowded open air cafe of wrought iron tables with umbrellas in a courtyard enclosed on three sides by the brick facade of an old factory. On its fourth side it faced the sea. Like Wyntonship itself the atmosphere even when busy was unhurried. A sign on the wall read "please, no studying during peak hours" but it didn't seem to deter the several persons sitting alone at tables from dawdling over their empty plates while Analinda and Maraqui waited for them to leave.

Analinda, hair in a short natural, an open top over a teeshirt, braless as usual, jeans and sandals. At five foot eight she was the taller of the two. While they waited and for several minutes after they were seated, they spoke about music, the menu, a current film, dancing about the subject on Analinda's mind. The waitress listed the specials for the day, repeating for Analinda the first two items which she had misplaced somewhere in her short-term memory. After a little while more, the waitress having gone off to get their coffee, returned, took the women's order and left them alone.

Analinda asked Maraqui "Have you ever been in a relationship where it just comes to an end? No big scene, no petering out, just nothing." She said casually, lightly. "One day you're standing side by side and the next thing you know the other person's not there anymore, like they've stepped off a cliff, like a trap door opened in the floor and their insides fell through it, right out of the bottom of their shoes. But their body stays behind. It's not like they're dead, you can still see them, you can still talk to them, but there's no connection anymore. Nobody's home."

Analinda paused briefly, thinking how better to explain what she was trying to say. "It's fine if they're around, it's fine if they're not, but you really don't care. The person you were standing next to just isn't there anymore, they now kind of blend in with the air. It's hard to explain, I'm not doing a good job, but that's William and me. I suddenly realized that I don't care one way or another whether he's home, whether he's not, whether we fight, whether we talk, whether we fuck, whether we don't. Zero, there's nothing there, nothing left, the glass isn't half full or half empty, it's been dumped out on the floor and run between the cracks, the liquid is gone, evaporated, the vessel is completely empty, bone dry. After all these years we're like two ships passing in the night. We've blown our horns at each other, as much to avoid contact as to say "hiii", and now content with the effort we're sailing off into the darkness and out of sight."

"To me, a thousand times in a thousand dissimilar ways." Maraqui responded.

To which Analinda replied, slyly with a twinkle in her eye, "My, haven't we been a busy girl."

"Well perhaps not a thousand, but I think I have an inkling of what you mean." Maraqui said revealing a bit of the coquette still within her womanly frame. "But never as intensely as you and William, never to the point where the floor was so solidly in place that I could say I was caught by surprise by the sudden loss. I've never reached a place where we've a shared a past, and had an absolute confidence about tomorrow. The first tiny tentative steps, yes, maybe, but I don't think I've ever gotten to a place where the floor boards have not been creaking under the combined weight of some new friend and me, where I've been able to stop waiting for them to give way beneath our feet." The two exchanged an empathetic smile. "What do you think you're going to do?" Maraqui asked.

"Probably nothing. It's painless right now. God knows what the disruption would be like. Maybe I'll have an affair." Analinda said broadly, jokingly. "I really don't know."

The waitress came over and refilled their glasses, the ice tinkling as it tumbled in the flow of the falling water. "I don't know." Analinda continued more serious this time. "I really haven't gotten to the point where I can sort it out. We don't talk at all. I think he knows, he must, but maybe not, it hasn't been that long since we've touched and that's all he really cares about anyway, I think." The low tones of her pensive words riding away on a stream of exhaled air and the soft breeze from the sea.

Analinda leaned her elbows on the table. Its legs a little unsteady on the dirt and brick floor of the courtyard, the table shifted splashing a bit of water from Maraqui's glass. "Sorry." A harmless disruption but slightly embarrassed and perhaps a bit insecure around the more worldly Maraqui, Analinda combined her apology with a rhetorical, mildly sardonic, "Well what about you, dear heart, anything new?"

Maraqui dabbed her napkin at the drops of water on the table and answering evenly said, "No." The topic for the moment finished, the two chatted for a few minutes more about the slugs in Maraqui's garden and the kill that she used to bring out the bloom. An insecurity aside, Analinda could talk to Maraqui about almost anything. She enjoyed her company immensely, finding even the trivial pleasant and in her own reticent way, Maraqui felt the same about Analinda.

The two women hesitated to bring breakfast to an end, lingering until Maraqui was forced finally to look at her watch. It was 11:50, time for her to go, nearly time for her to be where she was scheduled and expected. She caught the eye of the waitress and signaled her over. "Would you like anything else?" "No thanks, just the check, please." The women divvied up the bill and leaving a generous tip, got up and slowly walked out of the cafe. When they reached the curb in front of Suba's they touched cheeks, hugged briefly and said good-bye as Maraqui walked off to the right to begin her day of work.

13.

Analinda pauses, timing the traffic, before taking the risk of crossing the boulevard. Willing to engage in a midday game of dodge to stand for a moment by the sea-wall. And when safely on the other side and again at ease she will lean on her forearms and look into the distance. Out among the waves. Far beyond the garlands of sea-weed and algae floating amidst the iridescent bubbles of collected petroleum slapping against the barnacles at the base of the worn stone wall. Staring blankly over the water, riding the tide to the horizon until finally conscious of her inertia she will throw her body from its rest to begin the long walk to her house. In no hurry, weaving her way through the canvas stalls of the street vendors selling jewelry, and cloth, spices and food, and carvings in the market. And thinking perhaps of dinner, she will purchase plantain and salt fish to carry with her on the climb up the hill home.

Transport passes as she walks but this particular road out of town is not overly busy. She feels safe and picks up the pace as the slope of the hill increases, rising out of the brush that surrounds the tile roofs and white stucco walls of the houses below. Walking on the balls of her feet, pressing her toes against asphalt softened by the heat, springing forward with each stride, enjoying the strength of her legs, the flexing of her calves, the tension in her thighs. Taking pride in the fitness of her body as she begins to sweat. It is hot on the pavement in the sun. She wipes her forehead with the fingertips of her left hand, taking time to dry the moisture on the leg of her jeans, an opportunity to feel the firmness of the muscles of her thigh. Then shifting the bag given her in the market, she repeats the test, examining the tautness of her right leg, comparing it to the left as she pushes up the hill. The symmetry of her form is important to her.

Bumping against her legs, impeding her arms, keeping them from swinging freely, evenly, the bag, its contents visible through the pink disposable plastic, an awkward companion, it slows her down. Food that she would happily jettison if not for the need, harassed by its attack under the sun with her house still far away. Jerking her hand trying to wring the slack from its neck, twisting the bag to the left, catching it up, carrying it like a rugby ball under her arm, but it remains unruly, refusing to give in, loosening under the shape and weight of its contents. She tries again. Carrying it pressed against her chest. But little better, working for a few feet only before the bag revolts, the plantain and fish murmuring their escape. The three in collusion, elements from within and without, plotting a roadside break, the thought of its cargo tumbling in the bushes, rolling, sliding through the brush and down the hill, for a moment free, oblivious of the perils that might await. Anxiety and annoyance replacing the pleasure of the climb.

Having walked this way many times before Analinda knows that up the road about a quarter of a mile there will be a bench. And easily convinced that reaching it will be sufficient exercise for the day, she resolves to climb that far at her current pace. She will wait there for a bus. And so with this goal in mind her stride quickens and she soon reaches the bench, thankfully unoccupied, tired and sweating but in record time. She drops the bag heavily against the wooden seat, taking care to bruise its freight. And then sets her body down stretching it at an angle, 45 degrees to the ground. Shoulder blades against the top of the backrest, buttocks at the edge of the seat, feet crossed at the ankles, left heel resting in the dirt, perspiration dripping from her face. She pulls at her tee-shirt fluttering it as if the touch of hot humid air against her chest and belly might cool her skin, fruitlessly wiping her forehead with the back and side of her hand.

To the right of the bench stands a pole, a sign at its top with the number of the bus that will stop and the times listed on the schedule posted below, the schedule shielded from the weather in a plastic frame behind a piece of acrylic glass, as yet unscratched. Analinda has twenty minutes to wait in the sun.

She watches two flies play in the dirt a short distance away. Hot air lingering about her head, glad not to be the sweating victim of their affection, she leaves them alone, her thoughts drifting to the cafe, to Maraqui, to William, to the predicament from which she wishes to move on. The relationship that perhaps has become a mistake, a problem in need of a solution. And intending to think about what to do, she closes her eyes to ponder the options, but instead sinks into the orange glow of the moment, all her thoughts slipping away in the comfort and glare of the heat.

Until a car in too high a gear struggling to climb the hill opens her eyes. Blind at first, she squints, finally focusing on the driver, an older gentleman, in a white shirt and tie. He seems afraid to engage the clutch, scared that he might roll backwards down the hill and out of control, either to crash or to have to start again. His bony hands squeezing the steering wheel, pulling his body forward with their grip, away from his seat, eyes glued to the road ahead, he creeps past her then fades around the corner out of sight. In his place a car speeds by down the hill causing her eyes to turn in the direction of the growl of a diesel engine coming towards her from below. She grabs the bag and stands to wait for the nearly empty bus to pull off the road and onto the shoulder in front of her by the bench.

She climbs on board. A young girl in a school uniform sits reading a book, an old lady smiles kindly. Analinda moves behind them and stumbles into a seat midway to the rear as the bus in a roar and a jolt starts on its way. The ride does not take long. There are not many passengers and even fewer stops along the route and soon Analinda has disembarked at the corner and walked the last few yards down the side street home.

14.

Analinda arrived at the house to find the screen door locked. She pounded on the black frame knowing that William was inside intentionally trying to annoy her, pretending to lock her out. She pounded again as William came slowly to the front, and lifted the latch and pushed open the door. No, hello. No offer to help with the bag. He stood between the screen and the jamb forcing her to brush past him. “Where have you been?” he asked, his tone gravelly, semi-hateful as if the question ended with the word “bitch.” She carried the plantain and fish into the kitchen and took them out of the bag as William hovered nearby and asked again, “Where’ve you been?” Her back turned as she put the food away, she ignored him for another ten or fifteen seconds and then said simply, “shopping," offering nothing more than her disdain and the thought that if he were she and the roles reversed a slap might have been meted out as punishment for such utter disrespect. But she knew she was dealing with William and though not completely sure that all was safe, thinking it to be within him and growing close, she was pretty sure the provocation this time was not nearly serious enough for him to strike.

And her evaluation was absolutely right. William was too afraid to plunge his hand through the icy surface, the risk of releasing what might lie below far too great. He was terrified of being overwhelmed by the fire and hate. And so rather, in a pale parody that anticipated rejection, William pressed himself against the ass of her pants and in mock outrage and feigned contempt said "don't touch me." Of course true to form she pushed him away. But he persisted, pretending to mount her from behind, lifting his leg as if to find a perch for the inside of his thigh.

And for some reason Analinda tired of forcing him away, the confrontation settling into the past, she began to find his groping not totally boorish and farcical in the afternoon heat. His need, though underscoring how much between them had died, shouting that on occasion there might still be this. William as another being with whom she could have sex. And so in the end choosing to select from among the least active of the many options offered to her in Part Four, Chapter II of the ever popular handbook, "*The Cohabiting Spouse*," Analinda protested only mildly before dutifully, willingly, finally giving in.

He started simply at first, unsnapping her jeans, the back of his hand stretching the elastic band of the waist of her white cotton panties, his fingers moving nimbly through the moist soft matted hair inside. Growing more aroused he pressed his weight against her body forcing her to lean heavily against the counter, the edge of the tile at her spleen. And then with a jerk he pulled her jeans and panties down to her thighs, the cloth crumpled, binding at her knees. The force of the motion drawing her feet back, almost out from under her, exposing her ass to the air. The suddenness of the motion surprising her. His breathing becoming heavier, she felt him insert his thumb between the cheeks of her ass and in the crevice moist with sweat gently rub its tip against her anus, embarrassing her, distracting her, while his index and middle fingers reached down in search of the mouth of her sex.

Her teats still clothed rested on the counter as he raised the back of her shirt and flicked his tongue along the thin skin running along the course of her spine. She was clearly startled by the vigor of his attack and he sensed the role that force and vehemence could play. He sank his teeth into her skin. Jaws clenching violently enough to awaken but not pierce the skin. Not wishing to damage or outrage the nerves bundled in his mouth. Not yet time to require a defensive response. And aware of his control he reached up and softly pulled and twisted the nipples of her breasts. Until Analinda, his sweet Analinda in three long slow moans on the fingertips of her little puppeteer, signaled that the pleasure and convenience of his presence, for the moment had replaced her desire to be rid of him.

Leaning against the counter, breathing disturbed, head still confused by a pulse not yet normal, Analinda slowly pulled up her pants. And facing William, hugged him strongly, drawing the tip of her nose along his left cheek as she kissed it and slid her hand down to the front of his trousers, to his crotch, and squeezed what was hard inside. But there it stopped because to William the relationship had moved beyond trust and, at that instant in his mind, the gesture held a motive ulterior to reciprocal love. An attempt to shift the focus of attack, and regain a measure of control. He pushed her hand away, pinioning it by the wrist to her side, and kissed her hard on the mouth and then pulling away, assured her that the moment was meant for her and that he did not need anything in return.

Dinner that evening was a pleasant, if slightly strained, affair. Analinda, somehow able to make much from the little that she had brought in the house, the two found neutral ways to converse for the time that it took to eat. The experience of the afternoon unstated. They spoke generally of the news of that day, and of her art, and mentioned the possibility of taking a vacation. And after dinner they remained at home, William quietly to himself, not forcing his way into her space, even performing an act of enlightened domesticity, by clearing the kitchen. He moved forward with his plan.

To Analinda the evening seemed as it once might have been. She wanted to believe that there were reasons that they had stayed together for so long. And never truly having wished to confront the issue of how they would end it and walk away, she allowed herself to hope that it might be so again. Still she remained skeptical and unsure of a few pleasant hours, that were perhaps nothing more.

15.

In town, Maraqui has finished registering the sales of amber and silver jewelry for the day. Has said thanks to each of the happy customers, and watched as the last of them has departed to rejoin the colorful stream of passersby. As usual it has not been a busy day, but the shop survives. The owner is married to the landlord. She seems to run the boutique more as a hobby than for profit. Maraqui thinks it may be part of some unstated social welfare program. Jobs for the itinerant, or perhaps as a personal favor to her. Maraqui by temperament unemployable or so she thinks. Her idiosyncrasies generally inappropriate to the marketplace. But somehow her employ at the boutique has become long-term. The shop is quiet, convenient. It occupies her time without intruding upon her soul. It pays her bills.

She found the job through a want-ad. She called and over the phone sensed that she liked the spirit of the owner. They made an appointment to meet at the shop and the bargain was struck. Maraqui sensing immediately that the woman did not take herself or the business too seriously and the owner seeing in Maraqui a person she could like and trust. And neither having appeared needy to the other, over time they had to a degree become friends.

Maraqui places the day's receipts in the safe, turns off the lights, sets the alarm, and closes the shop. The street lights are on and lots of people are out in the warm evening, milling about, heading to the clubs. She is hungry and doesn't feel like going home straightaway. She ate a sandwich in the late afternoon, but it hasn't stayed with her. So she begins to walk in the direction of moderately priced food. Approaching, slowing, and then passing a number of restaurants, either too bright, or too full, or too..., always her appetite not strong enough to draw her in. And she keeps walking until after a while she finds herself nearer a bus stop than an eatery, and closer still to the comfort and silence of her home.

On the opposite side of the street from Maraqui a group of three, young men, islanders out for the night, walk towards the area from where she has come. Still in front of her, she can look at them without fully turning her head. They speak loudly, their conversation animated, self-propelling, rhythmic in its visual flow, but inaudible to her reclusive ear. An exchange in three part harmony laid down in a single perfect take. The young men pass her by riffing their way to lively up the town. While Maraqui responds in an austere single note held without pause until she reaches the bus stop, where with a twinge of regret at her back, she wonders if it all really is quite as bright and full and disquieting as she so frequently perceives it to be.

This is the Maraqui envisioned by William, the one like he adrift at sea on a raft. Floating, over and over and over again. Up and over, and over again, clutching the raft that forms the perch that clutches the back of every swell. Up and over and over and over again. Surviving without food, except the jerky that has become her skin, preserved and flavored by the clumps of salt matted in her hair. Up and over and over again. Adrift, but soon to land on a place that is green where she will no longer be alone, but with a man, a woman and a child, and she will walk with them through a park on a path paved not in gold but in the grey of freshly laid cement.

A place where to Maraqui's right will lie a hotel of individual bungalows designed to look like caves at the edge of the surf. A place, part of a town, where if she were wise she would not go, neither to rest nor take care of her health. A resort with a philosophy, not to be disclosed for free, and yet to be revealed to her in depth. Something to do with diet and spiritual well-being, to this point unexplained. An unknown with a cost which might seem to her so extreme that she would choose not to make the program her concern.

But she, along with the others, figures more shadowy than real, will go, walking on, past the bungalows, trudging on up the hill, the path carving its way to a sheltered crest where by her side a lake vivid and blue will appear. A large lake of which one day she will have heard much. And though happy to be there, finally able to see it for herself, she, the man, woman and child, first having to descend a sward before they can reach its shore, will be denied its soothing touch. Though not by the group of fat old men and women dressed in summer whites. The permanent residents, sitting on clapboard porches at the front of houses in a colonial style, having used their time to watch the path, about to be rewarded, eyeing Maraqui and her group with faint smiles, shouting warnings. While in response

Maraqui, the leader, bold but closed, not circumspect, will indiscreetly launch her group down toward the shore.

And the old folks will bring their wicker chairs forward to watch the show as the band of four approaches the edge of the sward and nears the water. A caiman emerging from the lake to the old folk's applause, a baby to be sure, but aggressive nonetheless lunging at three of the four members of the visiting party, Maraqui being allowed to watch in safety some feet away while the others become the object of attack. And the man, as a man is supposed to do, valiantly trying to defend, to distract the strong and slippery beast from woman and child will take the brunt of the attack, for a time losing his arm almost to the elbow. The caiman with its muscles contracting tightly about the limb attempting to swallow him whole. But the reptile not using its teeth, not there to chew and in the end digestive juices too weak to quickly break him down, ultimately will be too small to take him in.

Eventually the man will be able to lift his arm and swing the beast back and forth, back and forth, over and over and over again, until finally his fist balled up inside the muscled pouch will come free. And with his arm dangling by his side undamaged though very wet with saliva, he will yell to Maraqui and the others of party to stay clear of the shore.

But as if this were not enough, still her adventure will not be done and she will find herself at an open gate to an industrial site enclosed by a fence within which will be dogs; for guarding or simply wild, it again to her will not be clear because William will not wish it to be so. Four Dobermans and a single mottled, skinny, spotted cur. Maraqui on one side of the open gate, the dogs on the other and free. A decision to be made as to whether the animals will choose to like each other less than her. The cur will look at Maraqui and initiate the discussion. It will bare its teeth and growl. But there will be dissension among the group. The Dobermans will be a pack, the other a mongrel, perhaps smarter than they, but not one of them, and they will be stronger. One after another the Dobermans will sink their teeth into the side of the cur, warning it, wounding it, but not killing it. A concession on the part of the Dobermans that the cur will have a place amongst them but not the lead. And while this will be taking place the owner of the property, a woman in her thirties, will appear from one of the several buildings within the gated fence. She will walk past the dogs unthreatened and through the gate towards Maraqui who will not have moved during the fight. The woman will stop and with a padlock and chain, lock the gate behind her. And she will point Maraqui to a well contaminated with the urine of the dogs and explain that before Maraqui came the cur had led the Dobermans on a little adventure of their own, one which they had all found to be fun, a game called peeing in the water from which we drink. A prank for which the Dobermans had been punished. And Maraqui will learn that the attack on the mutt will have been an expression of the Dobermans' mixed feelings toward the cur, and a fortuity for her.

Awaking slowly together front to back, William will not tell Analinda of his thoughts. He thinks maybe he will leave their bed this day and seek counsel from an old man of whom for a fee he has heard can make that which one might wish come true. Of course William, not completely devoid of self-reflection, recognizes the dilemma for one such as he, a person incapable of impassioned selection, a pillar of stone not knowing how to move. And so instead of bounding to his feet, but rethinking what he might do, comfortably nuzzling against the warmth of his spouse, holding her softly to his skin, he hopes to begin his drift anew, over and over and over again.

But it is a new day and Analinda is not as fixed in her ways. She removes his arm from her side and departs the bed which they have shared pleasantly without further event since the night before. She goes to the bathroom to remove the sleep from her face. She crouches on the toilet, her bladder hissing in relief at the bowl. And then to the kitchen to put some water on to boil, where she will have an egg and some toast with her coffee. And before she can eat the phone will have rung and she will leap to grab it before it can ring a second time and softly quietly speak "hello" and it will be Maraqui who will tell Analinda of her dreams of the night before and how she saw young men who in another time and place.... And in turn Analinda will jest that there may still be a place for intimacy at least in her head. And for once Maraqui will not seem to take offense at the joke, but rather when the conversation ends, she will replace the receiver in its cradle and wonder if perhaps at last again it were the time for her to come out and play.

16.

William finally wearily awakening from his snooze sent forth in vain among the rumpled sheets a palm in search of occupancy and with equal measures of dismay and relief discovered through somnolent ears that he was not alone. As from downstairs a cabinet drawer slid to a close, and a piece of silverware clattered against a china plate accompanied by the smell of a breakfast made he hoped for two, he stirred to consciousness. He swung his legs to the floor and with the momentum gained hurled his body perpendicular to his feet in an attempt to jump start another day of give and take with the world and his spouse.

His first steps, really merely stumbles, his balance maintained with a guiding hand against the edge of the bed, led him to the bathroom where with dick in hand through eyes still closed he hit his mark managing to deposit little of his waste on the toilet seat. In keeping with his daily ritual of revival, he splashed cold water on his face and rinsed his mouth, and looking presentable enough yawned as he made his way down the stairs. And when he turned the corner to enter the kitchen to his unspoken disappointment he found no plate awaiting him, no extra food, nothing changed for his arrival. A table with his spouse, a couple of empty chairs, and the soft shrouded sound of a voice pronouncing him not good enough to deserve a second meal. With a nod he mumbled "good morning" to his wife. And she with only slightly more animation responded "hello."

Pretending that it was as he expected, and that all was normal and right and that he was there without disappointment, William stepped over to the refrigerator and pulled open the door where to his pleasant surprise he found that it contained some juice. He poured himself a glass and awakening to the day walked to where his wife was seated and with a jerk of his arm dragged one of the matching stick-back chairs away from the table to give himself room to sit. Analinda had a section of the morning newspaper in front of her face so he could not really tell how she reacted to the screech of the leg of the chair on the tile floor. But she did not say anything so he assumed all was still well.

He picked up a portion of the paper left lying on the table and starting to read noticed a public announcement in the lower right hand corner of the page at the front of the section that he had grabbed, a daily good word issued to maintain the moral fiber of the community: "Treat our children with love, kindness, and respect. They are our future." A nice sentiment he agreed as his eyes wandered on to another page where he read about off-islanders and their kids, tilling cesium fields and beating one another to death in their play. And peeping over the top of the page for a fleeting second at his wife he wondered what would have happened if, in better times the subject of a child or two had been raised, but always too busy, or too young or too financially unstable, neither had expressed an interest in the idea.

And then it happened, the notion of the here and now coming from nowhere. Thinking.... No, that is precisely what he did not do. Speaking without thinking, believing that he could say anything at all, William did not choose politics for two-hundred, or religion for four, no, instead he went right to dissolution for a thousand. And while pointing out what he saw somewhere in his little mind to be the irony of the juxtaposition of the sentiment of the day to an article on infanticide rather casually said "maybe we should have a child."

Analinda looked at him incredulously. Neither properly phrased as a question nor discernibly intended as a joke, the statement was simply, flat out wrong. It was too easy, he was throwing the game away. But she wanted to be sure and with a smile on her lips offered him a second chance, "What?!" But he did not get the hint. He was perfectly serious and repeated the words "I think we should have a kid." And now realizing that the king of the castle, William the fool, had broached the subject for her, her distress now relieved, the conflict from the day before completely resolved, she responded to his insipid comment without in anyway trying to soften the blow. "You're out of your fucking mind! I've been thinking of ways to get you out of my life, not ways to further entangle myself with you." And in the end, with the brief torrent of emotion passed, she asked simply, rhetorically "You don't have a clue, do you?"

And for his part, William now sensing that the topic was not going to yield any points and perhaps was not a good one to have chosen so early in the round, rose from the table and as if puzzling over the question, and without a trace of mockery toward himself or anyone else responded flatly, "No, I guess I don't."

17.

William's appetite having temporarily passed and not desiring to do battle with the little woman, he left the kitchen without further juice or food and walked back up the stairs and once again into the bathroom. He turned on the water and entered the shower, lathering his body under the jet of warm water and calmly amidst the steam pondered how nice it would be now and then to have the power to show one or two souls the errors of their way. Just a demonstration mind you, though one not soon to be forgotten. And because he would be benevolent, they, she in particular, would be granted a reprieve from the finality of it all, a chance to make amends. For William is not malevolent or vindictive and unforgiving, but righteous and good.

Well after ten minutes of absorbing the

soothing heat, his sinuses cleared, his teeth brushed, William emerged from the shower feeling cleansed and renewed, purposeful and true, and with a towel wrapped about his loins, reached for a razor. With which what to do? To lie in a bloody pool jammed against the bathroom door? To be discovered by Analinda while struggling to gain entry for her own toilette, assuming the obstruction a towel inconsiderately discarded by the user before, angry at her inability to insert more than a head and fingers around the door? There to her horror to appear slumped on the floor, a ghastly sight indeed, pulsing having ceased, stasis reached, just a trickle from the self-inflicted crease? Her remorse to ensue? Ah, or perhaps to run half-naked down the stairs screaming at the top of his lungs, a banshee, yes truly out of his mind? With left hand holding towel in place, right arm uplifted, a plastic disposable safety razor held high above his head, to tear and rip at her hair and skin? To leave her to be found, a quivering lurid piece of rejected flesh? No! Do not be silly. William has told you before, he is not dangerous. Good God, man! He wanted to shave. He had a washcloth in his other hand. A cloth still dry to the touch with which to clear a hole on the surface of the mirror on the medicine cabinet door, and as he looked at himself through the thin coating of steam, he felt strangely content and at ease with the inconclusiveness of his debate.

But he allowed himself to stand there before the mirror staring for too long at his reflection as if trying to make himself out in four space and his vision began to blur and he started to dream. And William found himself in a stone building where people had come for the baths. Beauveau as it is known is really a small castle, a manor house made of granite converted from its use as a private residence in the nineteenth century. The clients are beautiful and young and William is there because he is not entirely well. A friend of his is also there, a male who seems well adjusted and whole, possibly just visiting William or on a preventive stay, but from appearances one would think that the friend can come and go as he might please. Not quite so for William.

The two men are not lovers. The friend is clearly a man of the women, but he is by nature sensitive and forgiving, and so accepts William in spite of his peculiarities; at least to a degree not yet reached. So they are friends, William laughs at his wit, admires his self-confidence, and listens to his criticism. And after all old Will's not that bad to have around. The ladies find him attractive in a frail and ambiguous sort of way; mind you, one which he is not above cultivating if it will ensnare an occasional honey bee. Still, a person might question William's tendency to pat the curve of his tummy and measure its silhouette against, shall wc say a size 7, while furtively passing a mirror in a dress. Spandex in the color black, preferred. But as far as we know neither staff, nor guests, nor friend have seen him so adorned. That is, the situation remains under control.

Stepping through the French doors, this time unlike the last, fortunately open, to the courtyard where the guests have gathered, William exchanges a greeting with his friend and then attracted by the noise and commotion growing to his right moves to a bacchanal where a young lady pantyless in garters and white corset against her nut-brown skin has fallen splayed amidst the public dispute. William arrives, no attendant in sight, in time to look on disapprovingly, though not entirely unstirred. However, emotions cool as quickly as they have arisen, and the crowd soon disperses leaving the young lady on the floor, surrounded by William and three lovely young lady friends. William ever so gentlemanly extends a helping hand, but once the young beauty has been restored to her feet, he finds himself at a loss for words. Of course he would like his reward. But resisting the impulse to ask her straightaway, and with nothing immediate to say, he excuses himself. Oh, much too subtle is William in his way.

Landing back in the bathroom unscathed from his reverie, William finished shaving and returned to his room to put on his clothes for the day. Really not much choice there. He had simplified it to promote ease and avoid confusion. William was the proud owner of a couple of pairs of nondescript pants and a few cotton shirts. Once dressed which of course did not take long, he walked back downstairs and went out, through the front door without a word to Analinda who while still seated at the kitchen reading the morning paper was feeling considerably freer and less burdened.

Up the dusty path he went, not with a skip and a jump but still with his usual purpose, to the road where he turned to the left and had she cared to look out of Analinda's line of sight. William asked himself how could she be displeased with such an inconspicuous man? And although the answer might have seemed obvious to others, somehow it was not to him. Puzzled, he rubbed his head and then placed his hand upon his heart as if to assure himself of its beating and with his next step realized that in his rush he had left his sunglasses behind, upstairs probably in his bureau draw.

A staggering miscue which stopped him dead in his tracks. He had really wanted to go off without another word to her this day, but now this complication. What could he do? Go on into town and purchase another pair? A wasteful expenditure to be sure. Or be more practical and go back for the one upstairs. But the destruction of the drama wrought by such a blundering return. Quite a price to bear. Perhaps an entrance in a rage to cover his tracks, a rampage through the kitchen, a shouting match, but the upstairs part, it did not quite fit in the plan, unless she were already there. But alas, after much trampling amidst the dust, his feet circling in despair, it finally seemed more trouble than the worth and so resolute and momentarily clear, dear bold heart went forth, risking it, eyes completely unprotected against the glare.

To begin his day's journey squinting, vaguely aware of some danger associated with ultra violet rays, of the possibility of headaches and tears. And even mistakes in cognition. Conditions not unknown to William. He'd been down this path before. Found himself without his glasses squinting in the distance through layers of shimmering and distorted yellow light filtering through the bite of lashes locked together to protect his sight while unable to make sense of all the things he saw. Once, there was a horse in a man's britches positioning itself near a tree, standing on two legs as if to pee. Its leather hanging before it where otherwise a codpiece might be, only to completely disappear under William's hurried approach. William claimed it must have sensed his disapproval of such a public display. Or the time when he saw three men sitting together on a sidewalk, a spike in one of six arms, possibly the left one of the three. Though the image because of the light was fuzzy that day. But what he could tell for sure was that the needle still stuck in the vein had had the plunger removed. When pulled carefully free from the blue tube lying beneath the skin, the syringe without the arm attached was passed to the smallest of the three who from his seat with eyes bulging wide proceeded to suck the needle dry drawing what was left of the blood from the chamber as if some rare treat. William did not even bother to try to warn these three as he attempted to walk right through them and smash them beneath his feet. But again to his surprise they too were nothing more than air, distortion through his squinting eyes. And although it was sometimes hard not to be a little concerned about such mistakes of view, William tried his very best not to let them worry him.

With such things floating about William

found himself guided along by the gentle persuasive hand of the wind to the thought of how he might enter Maraqui's front door. Where with a knock he would call out softly "Maraqui." But there would be no response. And so more urgently, hopeful that none of the neighbors would hear, he would repeat her name, "Maraqui." And this time to both their surprise she would stand inside the door, and to his call answer, in a tone half-question, half-response, "William", but then say nothing more. Leaving it for him to explain his unexpected appearance at her door. If she had asked "what do you want," he could have said "you". But under the circumstances, only his name hanging in the air, she would leave the onus entirely on him to begin, to explain why he was there.

But he would not be completely without possession on that day. "I need to speak to you. May I come in?" He would say the words in a serious and straightforward tone. It would seem a reasonable demand to both concerned. They were not strangers to one another. In fact, almost friends. And the problems of his relationship with Analinda, known to both. He thought he might begin to build upon the common bond. Confide in her, to seek her counsel, until one day she would awake and realize that he was her girl, no, strike that, man, the one for her. But it didn't ring true inside his head. The role not quite right to his ear, not befitting him at this stage of his career.

Tired of playing sweet and demure he wanted a meatier part. Straight through the door and bang, right to the floor. Nary a word from her prone and submissive core. A real man. A pizzle with a mission. Cocked or pensile at the start. Not sure, but with the cost of film and crew not an issue, he could always order another shot. Granted, it might be a bit risky. The negative criticism and all, but to plunge his tip in that sweet spot, ah, now there was a happy thought.

But there was an alternative still. Quaking calm behind her paper, angry but at the same time not secure, feeling like a child evading a threat with a blanket pulled up about her head. A victor in the presence of the meek, perhaps not? So when the power of its black spiral spring, brought the screen door shut to a close, the sound though expected, still slamming her like a shot to the heart. She would pick up the phone, envisioning the speed of his feet, and from its dial pad, on her second try get it right, tapping out the combination of the selected keys. A bar or two later, a summoning hum, and from the other end, awake but still deep, relaxed from a full night of sleep, the voice of a friend embodied, to be digitized, now embodied again, "Hello."

Without protocol, no greeting in return, dispensing with the type of inquiry of one's health a person might ordinarily expect, but rather in a voice somber enough to be reserved for those times when the terrible has occurred, when one must prepare for the very worst, she announced "it has happened." A cryptic phrase of little value to be sure even when the "it", the terrible thing, is expected to occur. It was worthless here coming out of the blue and not immediately understood. To Maraqui's "what do you mean?" Analinda was forced to explain the drama that had passed through her house that morning with her spouse. She retold the events, disparaging him as she went along. The weasel this..., the little mouse that..., the dullard and so forth. The picture she gave of berating him unfolding with each sentence until the essence had been told. "He heard it from me this morning over breakfast, not in bed. I was eating an egg when the fool arrived downstairs with a simple thought in his head?" "He's a man, what do you expect," Maraqui responded. "No, not that, or should I say, just... he went further, in fact all the way. He proposed I consider having a baby." "His?" asked Maraqui. "I had the same thought. I don't remember if he said.

But assuming it implied and not wanting to throw fuel on a secondary fire, I jumped right to the main point, told him I wanted him out of my life, that the relationship is dead." "You didn't?!" asked Maraqui. "Oh, yes I did."

"And then he left. Just left the room, got dressed and left the house, silent calm like the eye of a storm. A few minutes ago without a word. I wanted to call. To tell you to get out, to run, as if in a movie, a call to my closest friend, but violence and anger weren't in his reaction at all. He just looked confused." "What do you think you are going to do?" Maraqui asked. "Nothing drastic, probably let him stay. He looked so pitiable that I'm not even certain if I could demand that he go."

And so although there was some uncertainty about the accuracy of what he could see, these were several of the scenarios played out in the dust and trampled beneath quick feet. William moving under the sun, back and forth, to and fro and in and out, Analinda and he, he and Maraqui, Analinda, Maraqui and he swinging from crisis to crisis as if on a vine, just a-whoopin' and a hollerin', as content as could be. Perhaps, or maybe just Analinda and Maraqui.

Or maybe the phone never rings. The call is not made and he arrives unannounced through an open window, athletic and lean.

She might never know. Bound and gagged, hands trussed above her head. Knives and candles. And what, no trust? Squirming, struggling to get away? Begging for a parallel life with no place to go until all composure gives way to paralysis and terror and fear before the liberation of darkness takes hold.

18.

William tried to imagine what it might have been like to have been given a bit more spring in his step, to have had a certain jauntiness in the swing of his arms, to have boldly possessed himself inside the house of his dreams. A house not of human scale and although lived in, quite unkept. Dark, dimly lit, seeming to decay with each step. A big house, really quite extraordinary in its size, and although probably never beautiful perhaps in its time a site of some geopolitical significance. Its exposed wooden columns unvarnished, looking now more like the roots of rotten teeth than interior enhancements, set split in walls turned brown from age and use and the accumulated soot which through the years had belched forth in a suffocating haze whenever something was put to burn in the thirty-four foot high fireplaces in the entryway.

The present master of the house whoever that might be seems willing to accommodate guests. There are several rumpled beds, although no one is around. Except a guide and William and a woman of slender build. The guide appears to know the house well. He says he has a room there. Distrustful by nature believing that nothing is free, William suspects that the guide may pay his board by giving tours to people he meets in the street. People he selects. People like William who go without knowing why.

Why the woman is there is equally unclear. She does not live in the house, at least not yet, and she is not with William, and the guide does not seem to pay her any mind. His attention, all of his energy, is directed at William, but the woman is all that William can think about, and he dismisses the guide almost completely from his thoughts. The tour of the house continues up the stairs to a landing where they pause to catch their breath and then continue up again to see the rooms just beneath the gabled roof. William takes in the tour through the corner of his eyes. Attentive enough only to avoid knocking into things, he remains ignorant of where they might be going, forgetful of where they have been, missing any detail that might exist. His mind lying entirely with the woman, so beautiful.

Her dark skin changing hues deepening to black almost blue at the visible junctures of her body. She is wearing a light dress cut low upon her back and at her chest. She does not wear or need adornment. A ring or two, some bangles, but nothing more. She does not wear shoes. Her black hair wild upon her head, flying up towards the sky like flames around a sable sun. He envisions being with this woman. Together with one another along the surf, her body, lithe, exposed to his sight. Or to sit quietly, comfortably in a public place and stare at the features of her face, delicately defined. To lightly kiss her small but bountiful lips. To unrepentantly look upon the curve of her breasts. To touch her hands, her long thin fingers. To play his mouth upon her slender toes. Her smooth soft skin. To hold her in his arms. William is in love with this woman that he does not know. And he is blindly certain that one day soon she will share this love for him.

He does know that this woman is not Maraqui, at least not the Maraqui that has come to his home. Not the friend of his wife. Not the woman who while far away amidst the heat and moisture of the rains of a land very green fell strangely ill and was never quite the same. The doctors said it was due to the bite of some insect, but others who knew said it was the medicine that caused the delirium and the fear that drove her indoors and ultimately away. She may resemble Maraqui, could be mistaken for her physical twin, but her fragility is tempered by a spirit still brightly fluttering, alive. A spirit William is quite sure is trapped within Maraqui. He will find it. This he knows. One day he will reach into her and as the master of the cage around her soul, open the door and let it fly free.

19.

"A new life for me! Please grant me leave to change, the power to be." William heard himself pleading from his knees. "What have you to offer in return for the powers which he can bestow? Nothing, isn't that true you miserable cur? Admit it, isn't it so." Pleasantly adrift a minute ago, everything had suddenly turned angry and abusive. Fire before his eyes.

Within seconds after the guide had ordered William to the ground, the Master of the house in a splendent robe and beaded crown, perhaps a distant relative of the royalty of Bamum or Kuba, had appeared without a sound. From a hallway. He approached the main landing where William had fallen to his knees instinctively, respectfully, quite naturally. Unable to fight, or to resist, he turned tail and ran from the urge to be free, without a fray he bowed his head and yielded suppliant to the denigration of the guide barking at his side. The Master, it seemed to William through prostrate eyes, loomed over him; standing opposite a huge divan pushed against a mahogany balustrade, there perhaps to prevent one such as William from falling to the floor below.

Its dark parquetry the only sight clearly visible to William's eyes. The Master's ankles rough upon his hands, he pleaded again, but was kicked away to the accompanying strain of that perennial hit, "Don't you dear touch him you worthless dog." Now lying fetal, on his side, clutching swelling ribs, William struggled to return to his hands and knees, afraid that if he were too slow he might be kicked again. In fact, his effort was only moderately successful but he did become a quick study, picking up the chorus to the tune right away, he was heard to intone, "Anything to escape the blows."

Truth now be told William did not dislike all that much what was happening. It was part of a tradition. Connately a coward he'd assumed the position before. Indeed, his entire life. What he disliked though was the pain. It couldn't be ignored, there quite unsubtlety in his side telling him much too clearly that it was up to them if he were going to survive, the directness of it all taking the fun away, he saw, at least from where he was sprawled, while acknowledging that it might be different for them, the two standing tall and pitiless above his head. Some words were exchanged that he could not hear. He assumed they were about him. He was curious. He would have liked the words said again. But of course he would not dare to ask. It certainly would have been out of place.

Silence between the two, William and the guide, replacing the soft rustle of brocade gently moving above slippered feet, gliding away, off into the distance, the motion stirring vapors, transmuting a solid to a gas. William knew it wasn't real. A trick unattended children shouldn't try at home. But he couldn't shake what was innate within him and call the Master the illusion that he was. So he stayed bowed on the floor waiting until he was certain that he and the guide were completely alone. And when the Master had finally and fully departed from the landing, his spirit no longer present in the air, William returned unhesitatingly to his feet.

William held no animosity towards the guide and the guide, no longer under pressure to assume a role unequal to William's, returned to his former size. The circumstances had been thrust upon them, it was all quite natural it seemed. Still, William was thankful that the woman had not been privy to the scene. "Will you be staying? If you'd like I will show you to your room" The guide asked William. "Yes, I think so, no wait I'm not absolutely sure." William responded. "Well take your time, there's no need to decide immediately. I'll come back in a bit." And with that the guide walked to and opened a heavy door, stepping inside what, from the outside to the untrained eye, appeared to be a black hole or an empty pit. William was left to think and sit, if he wished, on the divan on the landing by the stairs.

Well, there he sat for several minutes earlobes weighing heavily on his thumbs. Mulling over this decision or that until finally, unable to further examine the merits of the choices, in his thoughtful way having caught the cobbler by the toe, in essence having reached a precipice, he took a leap and with both feet squarely planted, palms firmly on his thighs, got up from the divan prepared to speak, but found himself quite alone. Alone in a house that was dark, and quiet, and unfamiliar. And except for the shadows, totally still.

Suddenly having come to his senses, appropriately afraid and ready to beat a hasty retreat. He sprinted down the steps, two, three, four at a time, until his heels catching the edge of a stair, he tumbled in a heap just short of the door, and ended up lying at the feet of something he believed might do him some harm. Dazed but aware he was dragged by his torso into a room. Thrown in a corner and quickly undressed, an ointment applied and put to the test, unfamiliar and largely hidden from sight. Which he failed or passed it wasn't quite clear, stiff and greatly confused. Perhaps not what one might choose from the menu on his first day there, but if forced again he'd no doubt submit, having no choice in the matter or so he might say. And who knows but with time and more gentle sheathing sufficiently safe he might even grow accustomed to the practice, perhaps finding it almost as good as he had feared, really quite natural and alright, maybe not nearly as bad as he had hoped.

"Please don't tell anyone." He sounded so scared. And the guide quite compassionately, rather than speaking his mind, chose not to rhetorically ask, "Is that the only thing you fear?" Instead with William cradled in the crook of his arm he patted and stroked his head, wet with sweat and asked from a far, "Do you know yet?" And William through what seemed like mist finally admitted that he wished to stay so he could learn at the feet of the Master.

But to the question "what did he have to offer?" he still had no answer. Though he could say to them they could do with him as they might wish, visit him as often as they might care to, that he thought he might enjoy, and if so, it would not be what they were after. The question to be posed by William and for William to answer was did he want what they might have to offer enough to perform more menial tasks, perhaps do some cleaning about the house. "With....?" He asked. "Yes, with your tongue at least once a day," came the reply. He paused for a moment pretending to think, to ponder his response. But demeaning as it might seem, there was never a doubt as to what his answer would be. He wanted power over Analinda and Maraqui that badly. A deal was struck. William, the new apprentice, was ensconced in the home in a windowless room on the second floor next to the bath. He learned fast. He did his job well and soon became a favorite who was much despised.

"So tell me the story again. Where are you when it occurs?" It was the guide standing over William. William naked and prone his head lolling to one side dragging himself limply back onto the cot that served as his bed, the sole piece of furniture in an otherwise empty room. Exhausted and near delirium, beaten and abused, he started again.

“I am in a marshy field walking on a board across a channel.” William’s voice was breathy, he was very winded. “Where is the sun?” The guide asked striking him in the side with his fist just hard enough to stir him back to consciousness.The welt, except for its freshness, indistinguishable from the others on the backside of William’s body. “The sun is high overhead in a blue cloudless sky. The field is very green. It is a field of high grass, but it may be something that is being grown, maybe rice or something, I don’t know.” William raised his left arm unsteadily in the air as if to ward off a blow. “Please don’t hit me? I am not a farmer. I just don’t know.”

“Go on.” Said the guide. The blow did not come.

“The grass or whatever it is and everything else is shimmering under the light of the sun. There is water in the field and under the board. I am walking on it to stay dry and to not upset what is going on in the field, not to disturb the things that are growing. Suddenly, as I take a step the board turns or breaks under my weight, I am not sure, but my foot sinks deep into the mud at the bottom of the channel. It gets stuck there in the muck and I can’t get it out. Finally it comes free but my leg is wet soaking up to the knee. I sit on a plank from the broken board laid on firmer ground and take off my shoe and peel my wet sock from my foot and there are two or three snails, inside my sock against the skin where my shin and the top of my foot come together and I know that they have entered me. And I squeeze behind what I think are their heads and through little holes in the skin, first like droplets of blood, no more like bulges of puss pinched from a wound, I begin to draw them out watching, enjoying, fascinated by what my body has stored. And in the end huge white worms flow out of my leg and my skin is left slack over the cavities where they had begun to burrow and make a home. I think that I will be okay, but I cannot be sure. I have doubts whether I have gotten them all out from beneath my skin. And you are there to comfort me, though I know I am mainly on my own."

20.

In a neo-brutalist construct designed to evoke the image of crustaceans laboring on the floor of the sea an exhibit is taking place in a gallery suffused with daylight indirectly transmitted to the space from above. The floor is made of narrow lengths of blond wood waxed to a high gloss. The walls are luminous white. There are no windows apparent in the room. The channels which permit the entry of natural light are hidden. It is extremely bright but the space is nothing more than a bomb shelter. One enters the building at street level and descends to the gallery via ramps notched by a series of elongated steps which do not conform to the natural rhythm of a human's pace.

Analinda has arrived to view the show of an off-island artist who she suspects is being presented as a result of self-promotion and connection only. The show consists of a series of faucets grouped in threes. There are lighted bars at the base of each work intended for the viewer to push, depressing the bars in any order or combination that he or she might wish to create a pattern, or a stream. But there is a catch. It seems the artist, a young man, very self-consumed, has no intention of permitting everyone in the gallery to be free to manipulate his art. An ambitious although little known proponent of the theory that limitation of opportunity multiplied by the sum of group resolve divided by individual caprice is predictive of value, the pieces have been roped off to permit a crowd to gather, but only one person at a time to approach. The opportunities limited, the consequences few, the artist proposing to use as assistants anyone assertive enough to interact with his work, he intends to employ the bold ones to initiate the action for the more tentative among the anticipated throng to view. He thinks he can awe them all with his simple little machines.

The artist is surrounded by a group of seven or eight persons trying to make head or tail of what he is saying. He's alive, animated by the sound of his voice, didacticism floating about in the controlled summer air. Alert, not distracted by his words, he notices several feet away that someone has gotten free. A viewer taking command, conceivably having fun. Two persons at a single piece of his art operating it in an unprogrammed way. He reacts quickly. From a table by his side he picks up a small adjustable wrench and excuses himself from the group. His movement is swift, nimble. He streaks past the viewer who has caused him to move and adroitly ever so smoothly adjusts the faucets, to the notice of all. There will be no challengers to the throne this day.

The show was worse than Analinda had thought it might be. The artist, a self-anointed priest carrying unholy scripture to those whose ignorance he had misperceived. An off-islander in possession of tablets no one cared to see. A missionary hawking rotten fish to an assemblage that will not swallow. Analinda wished that she had a hammer and a shovel to clean up the mess. She wanted to smash the faucets to bits before the artist's pompous little eyes in a performance piece not scheduled on the bill.

She started to ask herself why she had come but knew the answer before the question was fully formed. It was quite simple. Working night and day, not uttering a word, not seeing anyone, she had wanted to get out of the house. Slowly closing the door, leaving her hermitage behind, dragging herself to the surface, climbing out of her hole and for a moment seeing the light of day from the inside of a cavernous hall. She had needed to breathe different, even if polluted, air.

The gallery was only moderately attended and it seemed by no one she knew well. A mixed group of locals and day trippers there for the show. But in the corner of the gallery standing by one of the faucets, a young woman made up in black, alone. Charcoal encircling her almond shaped eyes, framing the redness of her lips, thin braids falling down about her face. An airy frock loosely covering her body hanging under its weight precariously from her shoulders. Analinda peeked at her, fascinated by the grace of her form.

The woman looked past the work before her and saw Analinda as Analinda peered at her. The woman's eyes knowing and assured. Soft brown against a blue white background surrounded by a fringe of long black lashes. A contact made and the woman approached but did not say hello. "This 'art' is shit" she asserted, her accent and mouth puking her disdain. Analinda smiled in agreement, observing the sculpture of the woman's face, its strength, the angle of her jaw and responded, "Yes, he must be connected." The woman extended her hand and introduced herself as Djene. Analinda, rarely confident enough to be so direct and always suspicious, usually held her own name tight to her chest, treating it as if it were a password not to be disclosed. But she was affected by Djene, the straightforwardness of her manner, the beauty of her face and form and she felt herself opening. "Your name, it's exquisite," she said. And then taking the woman's hand she let her own slip softly from her lips "I'm Analinda."

Djene asked Analinda if she had seen enough of the show, and might perhaps like to leave to get a glass of wine somewhere nearby. For an instant Analinda thought to refuse, her early childhood training having taught her to say no. But the reflex immediately passed, and without the slightest indication of hesitancy she agreed to go. Analinda lead Djene to a bistro of fairly recent vintage. On the few occasions that she had passed it by she had been intrigued by the sense of seclusion provided by the alleyway on which it faced and the trees overhanging its patio. It had always seemed to her a wonderful place to sit and enjoy a comfortable afternoon, a place that she had wanted to try, but until now had never found the moment right.

Analinda and Djene talked over port and Muscat well into the afternoon and in the end Djene expressed an interest in viewing Analinda's work. Perhaps it was this that finally sent William hurtling over the edge, and out into space, alternating between profanity, hatred and sleaze, babbling incoherently as Maraqui and the others would shortly see in an attempt to affirm his belief that his dreams were real.

21.

To come home, to find his wife's clothing strewn about the place. His wife and another. Two women in his bed, sweating, exhausted, ecstatically high. To come upon the scene and have his wife introduce him to the other. Without a hint of shame, as if what she were doing were perfectly natural, something understood and accepted between her and him, a part of their marital bond. "Djene this is my husband, William the Cuckold. Limp Dick, Useless Willie, say hi to Djene."

"It wasn't easy for you to take, was it?" Asked the guide. "No, it wasn't. What do you think?" Replied William. "How did it make you feel?" "I told you how it made me feel. Useless. They didn't need me in their ecstasy. I didn't fit in." "Literally or figuratively?" Asked the guide. "Fuck you." William responded. "I'm sorry, tell me more" the guide replied.

"There they were. Two brown bitches stripped naked under a sheet. It should've been a fuckin' fantasy. Two fine bitches in heat in my bed, but I wasn't even in the show. Not that scene. They didn't need me, not even as a donor. They looked like a fuckin' couple. And the fuckin' bitch, Djene, didn't even have the decency to seem like she'd done something wrong. She just lay there like she belonged. Fuckin' arrogant cunt, it was like she was fuckin' taunting me."

"So what did you do?" The guide asked.

"It was like walking in on two strangers making it. Male/female, three's a crowd, that sort of shit. I left. I couldn't kill'em so I fuckin' left. I went to her friend's house. I figured I had nothing to lose. I figured I'd walk in and tell her what'd happened and thought maybe out of sympathy she'd give me a piece. Sympathetic love. But it didn't happen that way. When I got there she wasn't there. The door was open but she wasn't home. But I had no place to go so I went in. Thought I might try to wait. Thought maybe she'd come back soon and we could talk but she never showed up."

"Really? That's not what I hear." Said the guide, trying to incite with just the tone of his voice. Pushing, derisive in his disbelief, goading William before turning to words as ugly and venomous as his. "I hear you fuckin' took her! That you fucked to her till she bled, till you couldn't get it up no more!"

"That's not true, she wasn't home!" William yelled.

"Really?" The guide replied looking William full in the eyes. Having gotten a rise, measuring him, assessing his anger, he remarked, "Well maybe so." Then looking at his watch and noticing the hour, the guide said, "Ah, it's time for tea. I must go. We will take this up later."

The guide pulled the door closed with a click leaving William alone in his barren room to think about his health and the state of his mind. A topic worthy of his temper, nearer to home, it was a place for him to begin. As reported daily in the news the incidence of Acquired Violence Aversion Deficiency ("AVAD") was up, way up, and clearly Willie wasn't immune. He had all the precursory signs. That's why he was there, though not where he wanted to be, needed to be, with a full blown case of the cure or, as some still thought the disease. But he was working at it, blotting out the regressive thoughts still creeping about in his head.

Sure he had a ways to go but at least he knew that he had lied to the guide. Aware even if only for a moment of the torrent of misogynistic puke that he had thrown up to cover the truth. The ladies had done it on the floor on the mattress in the studio. He didn't have to go in the house to see. It was all right there laid out before his eyes. Peeping through the window, the little man in his hand, it really was a fuckin' fantasy as he spilled his seed. They had never even known he was there.

22.

Marginaul is not a part of this conflict between Analinda and William. His days of the flesh are in the past. He is a dollhouse maker now. Content to be, within himself. Marginaul is working on the dollhouse for the little girl from abroad. A house for her family, complete with pet dog. A three story Queen Anne, excluding the basement, with removable gabled roof, and detachable walls. Marginaul insists that his houses provide maximum access for creative little hands.

The house will be surrounded by a yard, really a small hill, intended to provide a setting for it and to make space for the cellar below. After traversing the yard and climbing three stairs to the open porch the family that will reside inside will be confronted by a set of double doors, one screened and one quite solid. A step up, and upon entry through the main door the child will find herself, not yet in the house but in a vestibule with a tiled floor, a clothes tree standing to the left. Marginaul will place a summer hat and a light sweater there. He will provide umbrellas and clothes for more inclement weather in the vestibule closet to the right. Above the door leading from the vestibule to the house inside will be a transom in stained glass. The door itself in its upper half will contain a single pane of translucent smoked glass. Through this door one will enter into a hallway, a tiny rectangle of Persian rug to be placed on its floor, soft to the pads of the fingertips of a child. The primary floor will contain the entry hall, a living room, a formal dining room, a library, and in the rear, the kitchen.

From the hallway, a tooled newel post with a sphere for its crown, a staircase leading to the second floor to the bedrooms and baths. The house will contain five bedrooms in all. Four for the family and an extra for a guest or servant depending on the times.

There will be three bathrooms in all. From the bath in the rear, the one over the kitchen, a set of stairs will pass, running from the basement to the attic above. The attic will be finished and carpeted to allow children to play. Excessive noise dampened so as not to unduly disturb anyone below. Marginaul will leave the basement dusty, dank and dark. The walls rusticated and dappled, giving a slight appearance of mold. He imagines the little girl a bit hesitant to play in the cellar alone.

The girl he envisions much like his own granddaughter would be. A very happy child, well-mannered but free. Able to play and explore her surroundings at almost any hour of the day. Running, tumbling in the grass with her friends. He imagines the home to be nurturing and warm. The grandmother has given him hints about the family, the girl, her parents, the number of siblings, the pets and the like. But it is up to him to supply the detail in all matters of furnishing and design. He will create what he hopes will be an environment that the child will respond to as her own.

In this case a family of five at home in the country in the summer near a lake. Each going about his or her separate day. Gentle breezes brushing hot humid air past their skin. Life having grown relaxed, supple, now soft no longer passing at a wintry pace. It is summer time and the kids will be out from school, biking and laughing and having fun out from under the unremitting rules. And even the adults will be less constrained, enjoying evenings with family and friends unfettered in the late setting sun.

Marginaul has never left Veve but he knows much about life abroad. He reads ceaselessly, ordering books and photo journals to help him see those places that others call home. And from these he culls the details, the items that his clients so frequently mistake as their own. And so with the sounds and scent of cooking food and carefree conversation, the sights, a memory collected from a mythic time and place, spinning about his head, sweet-smells beneath his nose, Marginaul applies his awl to the thin wood and begins to carve a window in the wall above the back porch of the dollhouse.

The window looks out from the room where an older cousin might one day come to stay. Perhaps on a visit unexplained to the little girl. Or maybe the room is left for the purpose of storing junk not yet quite ready to be carted to the basement. Or maybe it will be cleaned and rented out, perhaps to a local student or visiting professor from abroad. According to the grandmother the room exists, that is all Marginaul needs to know. He will leave it for the granddaughter to create the uses to which it will be put.

Marginaul envisions the figures that will inhabit the home. The granddaughter for whom it is to be built. The middle child of three. A bright and happy girl who through circumstance and good fortune remains open to the prospects of life. Protected so far from the assault of relentless attempts to steal her childhood. To take it and remove it from sight, putting it somewhere far in the back of a closet to be stored along with all the other items that have outlived their usefulness, that get in the way. But she has been lucky. She is allowed to play and time has been made for her to sit at the table and talk and argue about the pleasures and torments of her day.

Anjou rubs up against Marginaul's leg and mews. Marginaul tries to shoo the cat away but it is hungry and does not wish to be ignored. Insistent in its plea, Marginaul eventually gives in to its will and leaves the bench to look for food to satisfy his friend.

23.

"Skittish and scared, mixed with a pinch of abhorrence and a big dose of craving. Woman as birdlike creature to be approached slowly, carefully, so very delicately in matters sexual lest one run the risk of frightening her off. A mighty powerful formula operating even as we speak." William was ruminating aloud, babbling to himself and Maraqui, his thoughts having seemed to wander off to some invention of a doe from another century. "Is that how you see us today?" Asked Maraqui. "No, no, well wait let me take that back. No, not completely but women, yourself included, aren't wholly ignorant of the benefits of that prescription, either." As William said it, he thought it a dangerous move, more likely to send her away than to intrigue, but he was feeling bold, with nothing to lose, willing to risk his birdlime he opened his mouth still wider. "In fact when the fear and the hint of loathing are removed, no longer there to be eliminated from the equation, no longer there to be overcome, when the female is just as up front about the need, the craving, desiring it just as much as the male, the mystery and beauty of the courtship ritual are lost." He knew instantly as the words escaped his mouth that he'd gone too far and lost his grasp on anything of merit that he might have been trying to say. His holly and mistletoe having turned to pedantic slime.

"That is total neanderthaloid bullshit" said Maraqui. Her reply swift to the mark. Indeed surprisingly so. William smiled warmly from within believing he had touched a nerve which to him somehow meant that she cared and then partially recanted his sin. "Perhaps you are right I may have overstated the point. Perhaps there is a different sort of beauty when the doe is no longer a fawn but rather an equal match. Still, there is something very special, almost tender yet very exciting about the young deer still struggling to find her legs, yielding, voluntarily, but scared in her surrender to the big horned buck."

William had finally called Maraqui. He called to arrange to meet. He did so under a pretense of a valid need. The worried, concerned husband calling the spouse's best friend for advice, a marital emergency requiring that they confer. It sounded sane and plausible enough to William's ear when he first proposed the idea to himself and still so when he practiced his delivery on the way to the phone.

But from there things began to unravel. The call did not go as smoothly as planned. He found himself frightened, exposed by the timid, suspicious "hello" which flowed almost immediately from the earpiece of the phone. Suddenly feeling all too obvious, he had been unable to plane the edges from his scheme. Nervous, he cut right to the chase, his delivery terse, a bit stiff. He did not improvise well on his feet. Still, it was apparently effective enough. For Maraqui, surprised by the call though not completely unexpected, was curious to see if it was as bad as she had heard. She had agreed to meet.

And here they were, together, with a chance for him to put his plan to work but as soon as he had opened his mouth he had gotten sidetracked, and gone astray, hurling animal imagery at her his first time on the mound. Not likely to win approval from the sensitive lady who, sitting opposite him at the table, was by now surely aghast.

Quite certain that he had confirmed all

reports of his behavior, William put the heel of his palm against his brow, placing it just above the bridge of his nose, and muttered to no one in particular, not even to himself, "idiot." William may have intended the gesture to demonstrate to anyone who had heard his words that he sided with them and didn't agree with himself, but it did not come off as such. A gesture of more import to the recipient of the blow than to the world at-large, it was an action so slight that even if noticed it was probably interpreted as a simple swipe, a stroke intended to relieve an itch or smooth a hair above his eye rather than anything to suggest distress or self-abuse. But for William sitting there without any hope that Maraqui would volunteer and not sure of what he might say next, it lingered much too obviously in the air rattling more loudly than the weak and insipid thoughts rolling about inside his empty head. And so they sat in silence.

24.

"Breathe. You've got to remember to breathe."

25.

From across the room came a wave, a signal of recognition which for a quick second William was more than happy to return. The movement of his deodorized arm designed to suggest to Maraqui that he was known, and liked and had a life apart from what she may have heard. But unfortunately the gesture was clouded by the reality that it was a wave to an acquaintance whose name he did not know. He tried to scan his memory but the controls were jammed, he could not recall the man's name. But as fate would have it the Gods were kind, sending him a reprieve in the form of a fellow who chose not to come to the table to give a further hello. Perhaps it was the way of William's wave, palm flat, fingers extended wide, a friendly smile on his face as if to say "I see you. Hi, how are you? Stop, stay away."

But an opportunity, however slight, ought not to be lost. So making good from bad, William chose to explain. "Phew, I was afraid he might come over, but he has left, thank goodness." "Who?" Asked Maraqui. "That is the problem, I can't remember his name. He's someone I know somehow from somewhere, but I could not introduce him to you or anyone else unless there were a tag around his toe. And I think I am supposed to know him too well to be able to ask him his name. So I am just glad he went away."

"Maybe he had the same problem" Maraqui offered. Perhaps just an observation, maybe even a word of comfort, but William could not be sure. The comment had not immediately sounded caustic to his ear, but a millisecond later he heard an echo which he interpreted to be doubt as suspicion's tiny feet scurried across the table. Who was sitting over there? Who could be sure? It would not have been the first time that William would have thought someone to be as simple and straight forward as he, only later to find out that it wasn't so. In fact, it had happened often enough that he had slowly begun to believe that almost everyone he encountered, could speak in a language that he did not understand, a language of innuendo and hidden agenda which he did not know, as if they were speaking a higher tongue. So obscure to his view that even if offered the words printed boldly on a sheet of paper with a Rosetta Stone by his side he would still lack the capacity to ever be certain of what was being said. And worse, he was never sure who knew the code. He wondered for a moment if Maraqui was one of them, one of the others, but he had no way of knowing, at least right then and there and the thought of the conspiracy hurt his head. So instead he tried to make a go of the interruption in quasi-analytical style. As if he were smart and had given some thought to what he was about to say. "It's strange to me. You know, a name? What's the phrase 'what's in a name?' Nothing. Some arbitrary sound I'm supposed to recall when a face suddenly appears?! Why should I remember his fuckin' name?"

"That's a point" Maraqui intoned. But again he wasn't sure if she was toying with him or if she really agreed. A bit of yarn in the claws of a cat. "Why should you recall his name if the association is of such little importance to you? Just to be polite, to be respectful, to acknowledge his worth as a human being, to avoid antagonism? That should be enough, no?" William did not have a ready answer, he hadn't been prepared for her to take up the charge and go on. But it was his idea to start with so he felt he had to venture a guess. With the side of his fist placed against his lips, his eyes darting back and forth, the clock ticking in his head, he thought the correct response might be "no." And so he blurted it out.

"No! No it is not enough. If it's not important enough by itself, then why should I expend the energy to try to remember a name? On the off chance that I might run into some guy, sometime, somewhere, and more politely be able to say "hi" and call him by his name?" The thought previously unframed but now out in the air and on its course made sense to him in a small but honest way. Unfortunately, a second or two after the utterance he realized that, even if true, it did not leave much for Maraqui to say in return and they fell back into silence.

26.

"Breathe."

27.

"So why did you call me?" Maraqui finally asked.

"Can we talk honestly, or will everything I say go straight to Analinda's ear? Straight to her verbatim or with a twist for a bit of added spice?" Asked William in reply.

"How do you want it to go?" Asked Maraqui.

William responded "I don't want it to go at all. Everything we say, even this meeting, I want to stay between you and me. Can you do that? Not tell Analinda anything without my okay?"

"No, no promises, I don't know what you might say. She's my friend." Maraqui was being straight in her response. She wasn't haggling. There was nothing to bargain over. William had nothing to offer.

"Alright, but give it some thought, please? My request is for your confidence, okay?"

"Okay" said Maraqui. A noncommittal response at best, but William accepted it. He wanted to talk.

"You asked me why I called you. I want to find out what you know." William answered directly. His subtlety quota used up, probably for the day. William tired easily and his recovery was often slow.

"Know about what?" asked Maraqui.

"About Analinda and me. About what's happening, happened to our marriage." William said.

"That's between you and her. What can I say?" Maraqui demurred.

"C'mon you're her best friend. I know she's talked to you. What has she said?" William asked trying to sound as if he were pleading, almost desperate, willing to try to do what was necessary to fix what was wrong.

"I don't think anything that you don't already know." Maraqui paused and then growing impatient with the conversation and warming to the task of delivering what might be a fatal blow asked, "You really want me to tell you?"

"Yeah I do." Responded William a bit of anger creeping into his voice, perhaps if he had been someone else the sound would have evoked fear or at least a bit of a pause. But as William was about to learn Maraqui was not the least bit afraid of him and for all her supposed reserve she had a vicious side and a sadistic streak, too. They appeared when she was annoyed and harassed by a feckless bore.

"She's tired of you. She thinks you're insipid, tedious and immature. She doesn't find you intellectually or emotionally stimulating. She thinks that the only thing on your mind is sex, sex, and more sex, and you rarely, if ever, adequately deliver the goods there."

Shocked by the suddenness of the onslaught, his troops misdeployed and overrun, William was left fuming back at headquarters, his mind twitching out of control as if he like some foot soldier had been shot in the head. Everything she said he knew to be true, but not yet fully ready to cede the initiative and lose control, the only response he could muster was to come unglued, or so it appeared. Spewing obscenities, spittle and poison across the table, violently false or true, either way not amounting to much. "Fuck you, bitch! You little lesbian cunt. What the fuck do you know? What are you fuckin' jealous?" Nothing particularly creative or in any way original from his mouth, just things he had heard before. And in the end after the ugly little outburst from the mean little fellow was through he was left with nothing but his ludicrous desire to throw her to the ground and show her just what kind of man he could be. To take the bat from between his legs and rip her panties free, bring the dolphin to bear, the missile on its target, to hit the home run and have her scream "Thank you, Jesus!" She was absolutely right it was the only response he knew.

Stunned by how swiftly she had leapt the fence surrounding the patch of civility in which they had walked for so many years. How abruptly she had started running rough shod through the wilds of his mind. Body and ego reeling, staggering under the impact, knocked senseless by the blows, and not strong enough to throw her down, he tried to clear his head but came up wanting, thinking only to ask what Analinda had really said about his skill in bed.

Fortunately, he was momentarily conscious enough to recognize how pathetic it would appear to ask Miss Maraqui such a question, especially while being beaten so mercilessly with her booted foot upon his groin. What a laugh she and Analinda afterward would have, the story of the bovine too dumb to defend, accepting all he was told and craving for more. But in the end he was incapable of anything else and so the words emerged from his lips audible to her disbelieving ear. "What did she really tell you about me?"

"I told you. Do you want to hear it again?" Maraqui responded with only the slightest hint of an edge, having dismissed his outburst, having seen him for the empty husk that he was.

"No, but what about the sex? What did she say about that?" William asked, the immediate past forgotten, now focusing on the intimate detail, not wishing to spare himself the pleasure of the least bit of the pain.

"What do you mean? Did she give me specifics, times, dates, positions, durations? No, just what I said. For whatever particular reasons she was not overly impressed dear stud."

Disappointed by the lack of detail, the absence of some falsity no matter how small to argue against, he noted that she had called him "dear" and so pressed on. "Nothing more? She didn't tell you how I used to beg, down on my knees, pleading her to let me dine and quench my thirst? No, too proper I suppose. And how about you dear, are you that way, too?"

Nothing to lose, everything to win. Perhaps the seed planted in her mind might suddenly sprout an interest not there before. A whim to give the otherwise useless castaway a try. A desperate measure by a desperate man to be sure, but he was unwavering in his faith in his plan, willing to follow it through to the end. Certain that he was on the right path and that she too could be owned. As certain as he was that he and Analinda were not yet through. As certain as he was that one day soon he would emerge as the master of the triumvirate he saw floating about his head.

And ironically it was partially as he believed, Maraqui looking across the table, her eyes stopping to take a good look at the shell without a brain, William the man. Although she had never harbored any particular fantasies about him, she had noticed that he was a man. Physically he was that indeed. Not remarkably so. Average, nothing more, but nothing less. A man in the same way that a girl might be described as a woman. His body possessed of the elements for procreative sex. His words notwithstanding, he did not appear to be physically less than fully formed.

Blind or seeing the truth, either way, it made no difference to him, William asked "What would you do if no one could see me now, if I were invisible, and I put my head under the table and started licking the inside of your thighs? Gently, no strings attached, expecting nothing in reply a moment or two of pleasure about which no one would ever know. What would you do? Would you make a scene? Would you kick me in the side? Or if

I were discreet would you let yourself enjoy?" William paused and waited for a response. Maraqui just looked at him. She thought of Analinda and of what had just been said and what she might say.

"You're married" a completely meaningless line. She was confused about its worth in the best of circumstances and as to William and Analinda, they were barely that. She nixed the phrase immediately. "Stop, Analinda is my best friend," equally strained. She didn't think Analinda would really care even if she knew. She certainly wouldn't make a scene. People would think her crazy kicking and yelling at a phantom by her knees. She did not have an answer, at least not one in the negative that she believed. Pathetic as he was, he was not physically grotesque, and intellectual and emotional engagement not an issue, she found that the proposition did not repulse her, at least not yet.

"Why not?" She asked herself if it really were as posed. Any overwhelming guilt afterwards felt, explained, purged in a confession, soul and conscience cleansed with honesty and remorse, an offer to do penance to be refused as a matter of course. And if the spouse did not understand, well too bad. The sanctimony of the reaction alone perhaps reason enough to have done it, and perhaps to do it again.

Maraqui was not immune to the image building in her mind. And even while not believing in William's ability to fulfill a pledge, she liked the caveat in the hypothetical posed, "no strings attached". A moment in time about which no one would ever know. A moment to be forgotten by the head under the table as soon as it had passed. She was surprised but could not muster outrage at the boldness of his words. "I suppose if it could be as you present I might let it go. But...." "Don't say another word," William said interrupting her from completing her thought. "It is as I present it and nothing less."

"Perhaps so, but not here, not now. You called me to talk of Analinda, the woman with whom you are having such trouble. Your wife, remember? So let's talk. Something you are apparently unable to do with her. Do you love her?" Maraqui asked.

"Do I love her?" William repeated the question as if he had not heard it clearly, or as if he were surprised by it and needed to buy some time. And then turning uncharacteristically pensive he answered, although not with a simple "yes" or "no." "In a fashion I suppose. I guess that sounds luke warm, tepid, but it amazes me when anyone professes unequivocal love. It makes me suspicious. I never know what it means. 'I love him with all my heart.

I would die for you. I love her, she's my life. I love him more than life itself. I couldn't live without her. He is my beating heart.' Is that the right answer to the question? Or how about 'I'd put a bullet in her head rather than let her leave me.' How's that for a response? I think I understand that one a little bit better, but it doesn't sound like love to me. So I come up short. The best I can say is yeah, I think so. But she treats me like shit so sometimes its gets real hard for me to know what I feel or why I stay. Maybe it's my love for her or for my own abuse? I don't know." William had tried really hard to honestly express what he felt. And for once he thought that he had had something to say, so Maraqui's reaction came as no small surprise.

"Oooh, that's deep. You really feel that fiercely about it, don't you? You big strong sensitive man." Maraqui, her eyelashes all aflutter, cooed in wispy awe-struck mockery before dropping the pretense. "Phhh, you're just making noise. Puking babble through the hole above your chin. Is this love or abuse? Please. Oh, boo-hoo."

Informed with a depth of knowledge acquired from his wife, her tone pierced William's chest with its derision, his shoulders slumping forward from the impact of her ridicule, for an instant he thought he could feel blood leaking through the walls of the chambers in his heart. William was beginning to realize, as he had hoped for some time, that quiet Maraqui was not as she seemed. Probably not the comfortable celibate of the past two years. Perhaps not even the reserved, repressed little agoraphobe he had had to drag from her home.

Recovering quickly, growing to like very much what he was choosing to hear, it was clear to William that Maraqui and Analinda had spoken about him at length. The woman talking about him, thinking about him even if in less than flattering terms, it did not much matter, believing as he did when it came to objects of his lust that bad press was better than no press.

Still, Maraqui's reaction did present a bit of a concern. Although William did not much care about embarrassment, at least not behind closed doors, he didn't particularly like it in the open air. And now here he was in a crowded restaurant telling all sorts of stuff to a table companion whose contempt for him was suddenly all too apparent. He had no idea what she might do or say next and it was making him a little nervous. Not expecting quiet Maraqui to be quite so open in her disregard of his feelings, so direct in her attack, hefelt somewhat betrayed, as though she had led him astray and caused him to misjudge her. And now not wanting a public scene, with her reaction to his reaction determining his action, the cart squarely before the horse as it were, nothing moved. Afraid of what might come next, he simply had nothing to say.

28.

Under the pressure of these complications William let his head fall back and took the blow, again. The punch resonating through his torso landing this time in the gut. The exposed bruised belly of his unclothed body. His legs draped over the side of the padded wooden frame prepared for his lesson. His hands pulled back behind his head. His breasts and nipples stretched tight. His buttocks suspended above the floor. And each time, right before the delivery of a punch, a voice asking "are you ready?", accompanied by a hand on his manhood, a yank, followed by an involuntary jerk as he tried to keep pace with his balls.

William thought the question directed at him but could not be sure since it really did not seem to matter what he might say in response. Still, thinking it polite, a query put to him, he would try to answer as often as he could through the pain, sometimes "yes," sometimes "no," but the result was always the same. The question just a prelude to the administration of a blow. Part of the rhythm of a song in which his body provided the beat.

And as repetition was the mistress of their mastery, each session would be carried on until William would find himself having little trouble saying "yes." And surprisingly, for all the energy expended the blows did not seem to inflict any permanent damage. With bloodless urine though bruised and sore, William was always able to walk on his own, back to his room, or about the grounds.

The guide visited William less frequently during the period of his beatings, busy introducing new guests to their roles in a house which William was repeatedly told was full, though he rarely, if ever, saw anyone wandering around. He would walk about the house on his own and never bump into a soul. Alone much of the time, his solitude interrupted only when he might be visited in his room, or summoned for a cleaning, or when he found himself in a chamber other than his own awaiting his beatings.

But those occasions were not the majority of his day. Rather, just moments punctuating the flat grey surface of his time.

Moments when shadowy creatures though of human form would invade his space and for an instant, maybe two, before the beatings would begin convince him that they were there to help. But he could never fully recognize them, never quite identify who had visited and who had not. And it left him feeling cheated, hurt by his inability to reach out. Feeling as if he wanted to send them something, perhaps a card or maybe even flowers, but unable to locate them in his mind or anywhere else he would find himself left during the rest of his day somewhat saddened, regretting his inability to express his gratitude. And convinced that Maraqui had experienced the same while away, he was certain that she could understand this. That was why he was willing to take the time to try to explain it all to her in so many different ways.

Maraqui sat quietly, watching William, scanning his face, waiting for a reaction to her words. For a while there had been nothing other than a slight shudder as he shot a glance around the room as if to see if anyone had heard what she had said. But after that not much more in the way of movement. He had seemed to travel off into thought, or whatever it was he did behind his brown eyes, leaving behind the restaurant in which they were sitting, transporting himself away.

William sat exceedingly still, very calm, a state Maraqui found not at all unpleasant after what had gone on before. He just seemed to shut down, to go into hiding, as if he believed that closing off would cause whatever it was that was bothering him to go away. A creature fending off an alien probe by going underground, or simply playing possum and pretending to sleep, not moving until the danger passed. It went on for a while, the silence, the empty stare, but blinking regularly, his breathing normal, she sensed no reason for alarm, no need to rouse him.

When he finally returned to her the first word from his mouth was "thanks." And then, "I have got to go, but can we talk again?"

It left Maraqui a bit puzzled, his gratitude, if that was what it was, sounding out of place to her ear. But seemingly sincere, more needy and vulnerable than pathetic as before, she agreed, "yes, we can speak again."

"And as to my other question?" William asked.

"From what I have heard so far, what could I possibly want to say?" Maraqui replied.

A question, an answer not leaving William entirely sure, he thought he understood her to have agreed not to report what had occurred. And uncertainty giving way to his desire to leave with a measure of flair, and not wishing to belabor the moment or seem too dense, he rose from the table and said it again, "thanks."

Having done it, having reached out, he left feeling so much better. Aglow, whistling a happy tune in his head. Perhaps not tonight, but surely further down the road, Maraqui would be his. He would call. She could rest assured of that. "Oh, what a lucky girl" reverberating in his skull. And ever calculating, the idea of starting over again repugnant to his mood, William decided the call would have to be made soon, while her feelings were still warm. The date had been a coup and to boot she had agreed not to tell. And with no confirmation to dear Analinda that William was quite unwell, he felt as if everything were coming together and falling into place.

Of course there was a slight hiccup on the way out, but hardly an ominous sign. As he was leaving the restaurant, as he was going through the door, just as his face hit the afternoon air he tripped on the single stair. Distracted by his remarkable success he had failed to notice the sign which read "watch your step." Fortunately though, ever the dancer, cat like in his moves, he did not fall. Just barely catching a heel, a slight hop, his balance regained, no twist of an ankle or injury felt. A tiny jolt and nothing more.

29.

William wandered about wondering if Maraqui and Analinda had ever spent the night together as more than roommates, as more than friends. Writhing bodies squirming, trying to merge, struggling to become one, fingers and tongues woven together, alive and probing, a tangle of soft curly reddish brown hair, mano a mano, pudenda a pudenda, pressed tightly against.... He realized he did not know the color and texture of the hair between Maraqui's brown and supple legs. An omission which he felt obligated to cure. Longing as he did to groom her hair with his flickering tongue. Perhaps it is barbed and black with highlights of red shielding the fruit that was soon to be his to refresh his mouth with and when he pleased. To place his lips around, and suck and strain the juices from its warm and tender pulp. Of course at first she would hesitate, the sweetest always do. Too embarrassed to enjoy herself. Ashamed to offer all her beauty to his view. But soon she would get over it and unabashedly learn to squat upon his quivering tongue and quench his flame, giving to him the juices from the sweetest of her lips.

And with such images running with abandon, recklessly, about his head, his throat parched he found it difficult to swallow, walking the streets as he was trying not to stare at all the women in their pretty summer wear. He wanted to throw one down and sniff and lick her there. A dog in heat, a witless rapist on the prowl? He had taken a turn for the worse and no longer accepting of the cure, he was unable to see wherein lay the harm. An offering excused by wanting nothing in return except for one, two, several, and all, acquiescing at his whim. The animal confused, blindly searching to be true, willing to receive as well as give. "What is fair for me is fair for you" fatefully carved upon his head.

30.

Maraqui finished her drink and paid the bill which happily was not much because William in his chivalry and haste had exited without leaving behind a dime. She noted the omission, assuming it to be only that and not intentional. William had seemed too distracted and confused to connive in such a petty way. Annoying, but not enough to be worth her anger, she let it go and hoped it might occur to him on another day.

It did not seem to Maraqui that she had made a promise to William not to say hello to her friend or in any way withhold anything that he had said. So as she passed the bar on her return from the ladies room and saw a phone she did not stop to ask herself if it would be okay. No, instead she stopped directly in front of it, picked up the receiver and dialed his home. It was not done maliciously, or secretively. She was not informing on a noble saboteur. No these were two women, friends sharing a comic moment. Women of regal bearing, two mistresses laughing about the antics of the servant class.

And though she did not shout what she had to say, there could be no denying that it was all said quite openly. She told Analinda of her husband's words and in response to Analinda's lack of displeasure asked then if it might be okay to use him once in a while in a completely dispassionate way. The two old friends understanding one another, a need being a need, Analinda did not seem to care. And so it was agreed that as between them it would be considered quite harmless fun, if Maraqui wanted some. It was really not as a big deal as one might have thought.

31.

"Awake, lying on his back the sheet covering his belly, chest exposed to the wind swirling gently from the fan overhead. Maraqui had just left the bed. Her feet padding softly on the floor to the bathroom, the soles so light in contrast to the rest of her skin, she slipped ghostlike inside and shut the door. William could not believe that his dream had come true. That he had been bold enough to call her again and that she had said "yes, he could come by."

He had wandered in the street for a while, he was not sure for how long after he left her at the restaurant. It was genuinely hot and he had been sweating and the sun was bright and he felt extravagant and thought how nice it would be to go for a swim in the sea. And having only his clothes and a pair of boxers beneath and given his mood, it did not seem appropriate to do anything less than to purchase a new towel and trunks. Something flashy and bright. So he went to the nearest discount store. And though a bit more expensive than he had envisioned they would be, he bought what he needed including, yes, a pair of sunglasses, and prepared to leave for the beach.

He caught a public lorry from the downtown to the shore where he jumped from the transport like a young boy. He changed in the bathhouse and then marched across the scorching white sand to an area cooled by the flow of the tide. A place to make his camp and spread out his flag. Not a rock or twig in sight. He surveyed his spot for pests and flies before arranging his things. Footprints in the fine moist sand waving good-bye, he walked slowly, steadily into the clear warm water. Mountains rising from the sea, towering over head, the power of the ocean here sheltered in a bay.

As the water approached his thighs, the gentle swells lapping softly below his waist, he dove head first into the clear blue water and opened his eyes to a swirl of bubbles racing past his face to the surface, leaving for the sky. A school of tiny silver fish turned and scurried away to his left.

William came up to the surface and began to swim in a slow crawl toward the booms floating at a distance from the beach. As he stroked the ocean floor still visible from thirty feet fell away soft and white. William took pride in the strength of his muscles propelling him further and further out to sea. After a while he stopped and trod water, turning slowly around like a periscope to view what might be about. He was alone, all the other swimmers closer to shore. He placed himself on his back and buoyed, relaxed on the surface of the transparent sea enjoying the lightness of his body. The sun warm on his face, bright against his closed eyes. He felt as if he were finally, happily, once again adrift on a dream.

A dream interrupted by a silly thought, suddenly questioning his distance from the shore. "Why was he the only one out this far? Did others know something which perhaps he had ignored? Tales of old, could they possibly be true? Monsters in the depths, lurking below, stories for children, no? Of course they were," he told himself as he found his reverie hindered by the thought of struggling against a cluster of scaly tentacles. Rising arrayed to strike, overpowering his unwary body, wrapping around him two, three at a time, dragging him under, unsettled by the sight of bubbles escaping from his mouth. William rolled from his back to his stomach and put his face in the water to see what might be swimming beneath. But the depths were empty. Nothing there at all but the silly image swimming in his head. Or so it appeared.

William tried to relax, to go back to where he had been, on his back floating without a worry under the sun. But the notion was not so lightly shook, and it drifted back through his mind, as he thought the beast perhaps very, very smart and not easily seen. He knew the idea to be foolish, but accompanied now by menacing music playing in his brain, the moment had changed. No longer perfectly at ease, he thought it might be best to return to shore. An orderly retreat but a retreat no less, he began to swim slowly back out of the sea, stopping now and then to float and play and assert his command over his fear.

William emerged from the surf brown, athletic and strong running both to look good and to keep his balance as the tide sucked the sand from beneath his feet. He had drifted down shore away from his towel. He walked slowly past the warm bodies beached on the strand in the afternoon sun. He was happy that he had come. When he reached his towel, he dried the water from his hair and brushed the salt from his skin and laid on his back to soak in the sun. His body made loose and pliant by the warmth playing about its skin, he wished that she were there by his side to become drunk under the sun and lose herself with him.

All doubt resolved, the sun relentlessly beating down on his skin burnishing the brown, he thought how nice it would be to turn the color of the darkest. A Wolof, Asante or Fon. But it was no longer to be. Time and civic affairs having taken their toll and the risks of such exposure too well known. Still, willing to take a chance, he turned for refuge first to his stomach and then back to the sea. And upon his return to the beach he sunned for a bit more before dressing and making the call to his dear Maraqui.

32.

"Don't be afraid. Put your thoughts on the table. We will sift through them together, just you and me." The voice came to him through the haze before his eyes with what he thought was a hand motioning to where it wanted him to place his head. To a table upright and spare. William looked from the hand to the table and back again, a request for assurance in his gaze and when he received it, he did as he was told. As usual the voice was not alone, there seemed to be others in the room. William thought it had lied when it had promised that it would be just the two of them. But he was not sure if he could trust his recollection of the promise and ultimately did not care. He would tell them what they wanted to know.

"It's William isn't it?" Asked the voice

more clearly connected to the hand. "Yes." William responded. He wanted to cooperate. He believed that he might learn. He saw no reason to resist any more. "Well then William did you go to her, to the woman, let's see, you have referred to her as Maraqui. Did you go to Maraqui?" "Yes." Answered William. "So what did you say? Tell me what happened. Tell me more about that day." So spoke the voice of his tormentor, his teacher and his guide.

William thought they may have taken him outdoors. The air was thick and grey, swirling like fog but it was warm. He would have expected there to have been a breeze if it were outdoors as it seemed, but there was none. And so he was not certain of where he was. In his puzzlement he had been slow to respond and so the voice repeated its command. "Tell me more about that day." He knew they would not give him another chance to respond. They would gladly beat him if he did not begin.

I called her from the phone by the bathhouse at the beach. She answered "hello". I told her it was me and that I needed to see her. That I was coming over immediately. She did not say no. I was surprised, happily so. But it would not have mattered even if she had because whatever it was, maybe the sun, maybe my daily lessons with you, I was going to go through with it. It took me a while to get to her house. It was quite far. But when I arrived I found her there, apparently too polite to have gone out. We spoke for a while, ate a bit of food and drank a spot of wine. And you know the rest.

"How did it end?" The voice, though calm in its tone, wanted to pry. It wanted to make him relive what he had done, to repeat the moment, to cheapen it some. "She cried." William said. "Do you think it hurt?" It asked. "No, I think it felt fine she was happy and thankful throughout." "So then why did you do her?" Asked the voice. "It had to be done, you know that. Why do you ask?" William responded. "Why did you do her?" The voice asked again. It was louder this time, more insistent. "It had to be done. You told me to. You said it was her. That she was the one." William answered. "Why did you do it?" The voice asked again. "Because I wanted to!" William replied, his voice in a shout. "Good, I think we have made some progress today." The voice came in response.

"And what was she like? You have not asked me that? Why have you not asked me that?" William demanded. "I do not wish to know" came the response. "Fuck you, I'll tell you anyway, whether you demand it or not!" William said enraged. "But I do not care to know. I do not want to listen to your tale." The voice was so calm and detached. So imperious. So full of reason. Its disinterest infuriating William. William who wished to be alone, suddenly desperate, demanding that it listen. "Aching to be scratched, stretching, arching back, palm stroking the hair on her belly, with eyes closed, her claws exposed, purring, then crying helplessly, just like the way she when out."

There was only silence. No response. William seemed to be alone. Had they left or were they standing silently observing, laughing at him? He listened quietly on his back on the cot afraid to rustle the sheet. Listening straining to hear if they were there in the room watching, ridiculing him. He grew certain that they had left. That the room was empty. That he was really alone. But still he was afraid to draw a breath. Afraid that any sound he might make, any sound at all, might bring their attention back to him. He lay there still, immobile, as if safe in the room where they had been an instant before. It was still somehow not clear to him that they knew exactly where to find him, and that he was always in their thoughts even if he did not make a sound.

He laid there for a while in the dark. There in the room without a window. The room without sight. The little light that may have existed having left with the departure of his visitors. He lay there silently, still, sapped of all energy. Consciousness returning to him like the motion of the tide. Sweeping over him briefly, depositing itself in his mind and then receding from memory, teasing him with its presence then leaving him behind. It came to him over and over again in a rhythm of its own. And very gradually, imperceptibly at first, like oxygen filling the deepest recesses of his lungs, it caused his brain to start to function once again and with it a bit of his will returned and after the passage of a great deal more time, he began to regain control over the use of his limbs.

He peeled his back from the sheet and tested his legs, moving slowly toward the door that he recalled having seen before. A single door made of wood embellished with recessed panels rectangular in form and covered with flaking shellac, he reached out, cautiously touching, but not trying the knob. The touch apparently enough, he sensed that the room was unlocked, and except for the suddenly not insignificant worry that he did not know what or who he might face if he entered the corridor on the other side, he seemed free to go. He listened intently by the door for footsteps or commotion, the breathing of a friend or a foe, unsure if it were worth the risk. And counting the reasons why not to leave, he realized that he did not even know if there were a corridor on the other side. He had never actually walked to the room. He had always arrived unconscious, having been carried there. Each session starting and ending without consciousness on either side. A before and after reconstructed only later when he would find himself elsewhere. And now thinking seriously that there might be nothing on the other side of the door but the cold howling wind, he paused and rubbed his forehead uncertain about what to do. Not sure whether to try to return to the safety of the cot, or to stay where he stood on a plank in the floor, or to test his mettle and open the old wooden door from the room.

William emboldened by reasons unknown to him, less tentative than before, grasped the dented brass knob in the soft palm of his right hand and turned it round and round, but it did not catch. The tongue of the lock not retracting from its groove in the jamb. It would not let go of its hold. He tried again turning the knob first to the right then to the left and then back and forth until finally, slowly it began to resist and the door came free in his hand. He pulled it very gently at first afraid that whatever might be outside was waiting to rush in. Afraid that he would be overwhelmed. But then for no reason at all, for he had never noticed her to have been there before, he thought that Analinda might be on the other side of the door, out there waiting for him. Waiting to take him in her arms, to hold him tight against her breast and keep him warm.

But then he thought it could be worse, and that she too might be in danger. So heedless of the peril, forgetting all that had gone before, he boldly threw open the door only to find that his first thought had been right. There was nobody there. No one at all. He stood naked and completely alone enveloped in darkness in an empty house. The scant light of the corridor and the blackness from the room mixing together to form the night.

Frightened and now in a panic William fell to his knees afraid that the floor might suddenly end, that he might fall and continue to fall and not stop until his heart raced finally out of control. He much preferred to be naked on his knees pointing limply toward the floor than to be found standing. The image distended by the thought of the position William found himself willing to be alone no more. He hoped to be summoned once again. He began to crawl slowly about on all fours putting forth his nose and jaws to show that he was the one. The only person in the house right for the job at hand. William who would remake himself for the pleasure of their company, would give them his silky tongue. Who were these persons who held such sway? The faceless souls that controlled him night and day? He grabbed his temples as if to scream, as if the noise might help him focus and form a picture of their faces in his mind, but no sound escaped, his mouth open, agape, without a cry. And so empty, without support, neither theirs nor hers, he placed his palms back on the floor, down again amongst the dry heaves of the wretched who had passed that way before.

33.

Analinda had never been with a woman before. She had thought of the possibility, not frequently, but often enough, on occasion walking along the quay or in a leisurely moment at home, but she had never committed the deed, never actually been to bed with one the same as she. She guessed the circumstances had never been right. Lacking anonymity, maybe not just really attractive enough, or as with her thoughts of the possibility with Maraqui always complicated by the state of her relationship with her spouse. But with Djene none of this had come into play. The moment had been right, everything had been aligned and somehow for a moment in time she had let it happen and it was as she had dreamed it might be. She had let herself go and for the first time in her life, for an instant, brief as it was, felt totally free and at ease, completely willing, powerless to resist, she screamed at the top of her lungs and was born in an explosion of light.

And when it was over, when she was conscious of having come back to the room and the bed in which they lay and her breathing had returned almost too normal Analinda realized that she had forgotten her spouse, lost as she had been. She had no doubt that it would not have been the same. If the other had been a man. To compare his feel, his touch or smell. But it had been so very different with this person of similar body. There had been nothing to compare, nothing to distract her from where she wished to go. For the first time she had found herself disentangled and free. Ever so briefly free, released from thought, any thought at all. It was all so very new, so beautiful, not to be suddenly drawn away. To pass beyond the usual, the modicum of pleasure she had grown to know, but instead to be lost in the other and for a flash, an instant in time, perfectly situated, at one with herself, the other and her mind.

34.

"For a second before the envy went away and the rage fully took control, I think I was truly happy for her, there in her ecstasy. For a second I think I loved her that much. But it turned so quickly when I saw them laughing at me. I told this all to Maraqui. And I told her more. I told her that I would have thought if anyone it would have been her, that she would have been the one to have done it to me. And I asked her if they had. But she denied it. And then in a voice that seemed genuine and very honest she said 'It is funny though, as you tell it, I don't quite know how I feel. Maybe a little rejected too.' I liked her at that moment when it appeared that somewhere not too deep inside she had probably wanted to. But apparently they never spoke in those terms."

35.

Djene propped herself uncomfortably on an elbow and looked about the studio. Her eyes coming to rest on the work of the family in progress. Leaning as she was, the joints of her shoulder and neck started to hurt under the weight of her body. She sat up to get a better view of the sculpture, drawing her knees to her chest for balance, rocking slowly, almost imperceptibly from side to side on her buttocks and heels. She wondered what might have inspired the work. The jaggedness of its anger disturbed her in a way that she liked.

She recalled the story of a little girl in the States who one day went berserk, attacking her brother and two sisters with a gun. The two sisters were able to find refuge in a storage room which the bullets were unable to penetrate. However, when the brother tried through a side door to gain entrance to the room the girls mistook him for the crazed sibling and shot him dead with a weapon they had grabbed for their defense. The children, the oldest of whom was ten, were apparently well schooled in the art of violence. It was one of those momentary tragedies which slip gently into place in the background amidst the other items that make up the daily roar. The sculpture reminded her of how she had felt when she first heard the story.

"I would like to show that piece in my gallery. May I?" Djene asked. "You own a gallery? Analinda asked sounding a little surprised. Djene had referred to it only as a business without elaborating when the women had spoken of work earlier at the bistro. "Is that why you were at the show?"

"Yes, I have come for a brief vacation and to see what's current here. I like your work very much." Said Djene.

"Thank you. But unfortunately that piece is already committed, but maybe we can do something together in the future." Analinda responded laughing at the notion of conducting the art of business as they were, naked beneath a sheet in the late afternoon. And Djene in an unsolicited and genuine tone of voice that was offered to allay any suspicion which might have crept forth under the circumstances said, "This is truly new for me."

The women found that they liked one another very, very much. There was an ease, an informality between them as if they were old friends. Djene leaned over and kissed Analinda lightly on the lips. Then she stood up and asked if she could get something to drink. Analinda said "yes" and directed her to the kitchen and watched as she walked away. Then she lay back on the futon and enjoyed the feeling coursing through her mind.

36.

You seem like a fly on the wall. And I think you like your status as such. Watching your wife and others play. Watching them live. Watching them learning to enjoy themselves. You get off on it don't you?" It was the guide having stopped by for a chat, asking William if he might like to further torment himself. And William who had found his way back down the hall and ensconced himself safely once again in his room had been more than happy to oblige when the guide had come a rapping at the door. In his present state of mind William found himself most willing to let the tale unfold. He was on a roll now uttering every word upon command, slathering humiliation with his tongue about his cheeks, on his lips, and jaws. He was happy to tell the truth, happy to get it out.

William sat up suddenly, sweat pouring from his head, falling in droplets from his nose. He had drifted off despite his best effort not to. He had desperately fought to stay awake to keep from losing consciousness but his eyes had started burning and the motion of the waves had all been too much and ultimately he had lost any belief that it might matter so he had let himself sink and slip away. Drifting, drifting gradually softly down, without concern for life or limb, fingers hanging overboard tickling the salt floating on the surface of the sea. He had tucked himself ever so gently in the comfort of her arms.

But awakened by a change, something in the air, or perhaps the rush of the water against his hand, he was once more suddenly aroused, shaken, terrified of her embrace. He fought against her, valiantly playing number games in his mind, but it was always just a matter of time, her caress so natural. Eventually he had to rest his head, she knew this and could wait. And after a minute or two, unable to resist, he laid himself gently down. And just as he had feared she returned to him, her arms so soft, their warmth so sweet.

The dreams came in a swirl, sucking him down, deep into their clutches where over and over they caught him trying to escape. They would throw him down or hold him against a wall and beat him again. He raised his hands up about his head to protect his eyes, nose, and face only to expose his belly and below. And helpless to oppose the shift in focus he would double over under their attack. A torture of one, unable to call for aid. And after many days of such repeated joy he begged to be allowed to die. But they refused him his request and would not let him slip ultimately away. Not yet his time, naked without tools in a padded cell to be fed intravenously if it came to that one day.

Never one given to religion still once he tried to will himself away, to disperse his energy throughout the universe first with prayer and when that did not succeed.... But for reasons beyond his ken nothing seemed to work. And he was left to wonder why he was required to remain day in and day out while others seemed allowed to flee.

He was permitted nothing of his own during these sessions and as for anything he might attempt to call his own, he was quickly disabused of his mistake, time and again shown that whatever it might be was not his to possess. Of the voice and the others who came to visit he would say "everything is yours, nothing is mine, you are everything." It was a mantra he was taught, and obediently learned, silently without thinking, repeated over and over again.

Though it was now all very vague, William remembered being away from home, away from Veve, driving a vehicle up a steep grade. The car barely climbing the hill. Moving, but achingly slow. Struggling to proceed. About two-thirds of the way up the grade William came upon a disturbance, still up ahead a few yards away but closing the gap with each foot he moved. A man arguing with the police. Angry, belligerent, undeterred by the uniforms or authority they purported to represent. William recognized that his way was about to be blocked, his progress stopped by the mini-battle. A fight that few, if any, would ever hear about. Sure that he would be caught up in the battle if he reached it, and even more certain that if he reached it he would never move forward again, and convinced that the battle was not his own, he tried to turn the car around and go back in the direction from which he had come. But his maneuvering not as swift as he would have liked, he suddenly found himself a would-be accomplice in the man's escape. The vehicle slow to pick up speed, the man saw his chance. Breaking free from the police, he ran after William, steadily gaining ground his fingers only inches from grabbing hold of the chrome handle to the right rear door.

William understanding the man to be

a fugitive from the law, and dangerously so, tried to push the button to lock the door and at the same time drive away. But he was not very successful at either. Proving difficult to secure, and with the car, though weaving and almost out of control, about as slow in its descent as it had been in its climb, William was able to get the door locked just in the nick of time. The man's face now pressed against the glass pounded the window with his fist while screaming at William to let him in. But William was scared and continued on his way until finally the car picked up enough momentum to force the man to let go. And as his running slowed but before he really began to fade the man screamed at William to stop and said something more. Throughout the ordeal William had kept turning his sight back and forth from the road straight ahead to the increasingly panicked fugitive at his right rear door, at times looking the man dead in the face. And so when at last the chrome had been ripped from the fugitive's hand and the chase had entered its final stage William knew that the man had meant it when he shouted, "I'll nail your ass to a wall you coward, you bastard, you whore!"

For days after the event William saw the man's face wherever he turned. He saw the man coming to meet him while walking alone on the street. He saw the man while shopping in the local store for something to eat. He saw the man standing behind him while inspecting his own face in the mirror on the bathroom wall. The face of the man, obsessed and consumed with hatred, waiting for him. William told this story to two others who shared his fear. The oddity of the coincidence neither questioned nor understood. Two whom he had met in the street. Two whom he had not met before, not otherwise friends, simply drawn to each other by terror and fear and a common betrayal.

The three quickly realized that the fugitive was not an ordinary man, not human in the usual sense. Incapable of exhibiting the feelings they so desperately wished to receive. It was clear to them that he could neither forgive nor forget. His malice unambiguous, his soul completely bereft, insensitive to their plight, he would pursue them until they were dead. The three knew he had to be killed. They set out to decapitate him with a sword. Yes, that was their total plan, not even a trap. But as luck would have it the man stumbled into their midst, really they were just standing together in a basement when he walked in. Dumb luck, nothing more. Just good fortune, an armament and numbers on their side.

They sat him in a chair, as one of the three

held him while another bound him with a rope around his arms and legs tied much too tight just to hold him there. Tight enough to cut the flow of blood and turn his limbs blue. Tight enough to make him suffer. It was William's job to expose the man's neck to the blade. A task for which William felt eminently qualified. With his left hand William pulled taut the hair on the man's head and with his right hand cupped his chin, raising it in the air. The Adam's apple of the man stretched and bobbing with each swallow of fear as the third of the brave band wielded the sword. With a precise swipe of the blade he cut right through the layer of, shall we call it, skin and clean through the jugular stopping with a scratch of the spine. "Not so big and bold now are you?" They laughed.

But their laughter soon stopped. There was surprisingly little blood and much of what was there was already dry as if the execution had happened before. The men rubbed their eyes and looked again realizing that what they had cut was not of humankind, but rather a plaster of Paris cast of a man. The fugitive they wanted to kill, seated next to them, head still quite intact and in a manner of speaking very much alive. It was at that moment that William and the other two knew. It was not their assailant but they who were about to die.

But at the very moment when all seemed lost and the others stood in a complete state of despair, William shook his fist in the air and fought to regain control. Not to be overtaken by the event, for the first time in years William rose to his full height, which in heels on a good day could find him standing five foot two. Except for a number of fears, lack of strength and aversion to speed William had always hoped to ride a great steed in one of the famous derbies of the world. But that had yet come to pass and since he was feeling that an opportunity to strike a blow for freedom, admittedly only that of his own and the other two, was then at hand, he took the chance and fought the fugitive man.

What brass, what balls William displayed that day as the blood flowed from his wounds. Valiantly plodding forward, never in retreat but despite his best effort not close to a match. In the end trying only to cuddle himself near where he lay. It was unclear in his mind, really just a blur, how many times he had been knocked from his feet. He thought it may have been seven or eight before he had been forced to stay down, but he could never really be sure because although much like William's stature in breadth of time, it had been by any standard an exceedingly nasty fight. Short but not sweet, in the bat of an eye he was knocked off his feet, picked up and thrown down again and again. Poor William who had not so much as landed a single punch would later find what little was left of himself, defenseless and fetal, beaten and this time not even able to crawl.

37.

William had no recollection of what became of the other two. They seemed to have slipped from his memory. Like so many other painful events, sometimes here, sometimes there, sometimes pieced together in a meaningful way, sometimes lost depending on the hour of the day. Only a rough idea of what was true. Drifting alone in his head, taking refuge in his dreams, that much he knew.

An hour before it had all seemed so safe. Nowhere near the place he had been warned not to go. Not out sightseeing, not a tourist or voyeur, not in the east end of town or anywhere else for that matter. Far from the few houses that remained standing. Not out walking and never in the midst of the charred ruins that the arsonists called home. When this all occurred, on a Sunday no less, he had been safely ensconced in a chair on the deck. Not on the prowl as he had once let it be known. When it was time to stroll in the heat and the sun and sweat with the local citizenry out on display he had been asleep, shadowless in the afternoon. William was not the one driving his car on a lonely stretch of road flat and gently curved when another primed in grey in need of a second coat stopped by the curb to belch smoke and noise from the passenger's side without a cop in sight. It was just William and another local, who vocal as they were, in the end really did not matter to anyone all that much. And no longer knowing, unable to remember any of this very well, he didn't seem to care. It was all just running through his head. A swirl of random thoughts about things probably better left unsaid.

Like the old woman in the chair next to him, just ranting again. Telling the story of how when she was young the machines had come one day to take her away. How they had monitored her brain and ruined her life and now certain of the identity of the orderly, shouted "You're one of them! Don't think I don't know!" The old lady demanding to be told, asking "Why'd you bring me here? What do you want?"

And the orderly's reply, not good enough, too slow "Just taking you for some air, Ma'am.

We do this every day." An answer so calm and pacific that it set her off. Ashy grey and yellow eyed, skeletal thin in a pink robe with white piping wearing buckskin fleece lined slippers ankle high in the ninety degree heat, she started to bellow again. "All the years I've been here you've never taken me out for air! Why now? What are you gonna do?" The old hag pausing for a while looking inward as if resigned, then either forgetting or feeling refreshed, William could never be sure, she started anew, noisy but not yet at the top of her lungs, not so loud as to require more from the orderly who having learned to ignore her was now absorbed with the magazine he held in his lap. "You're one of them! Don't think I don't know!"

But William was not so immune. For him, the ranting, it really disturbed his mood. And feeling no kinship to her at all, he wanted her removed. The old lady, the crone, the crazy old whore. "Roll her away!" He wanted to say but he knew it unwise. Most likely just set her off, get her going again. The old bat, flying about, puking her past all over his sea and his sun, making it impossible for him to forget where he was. Anyway she seemed to be tiring and quieting down. Probably soon stop on her own. But he wasn't positive, not absolutely sure, so he prayed in his head, quickly, silently murmuring to himself over and over and over again, "Please be quiet, please be quiet, please...."

www.ingramcontent.com/pod-product-compliance
Lightning Source LLC
Chambersburg PA
CBHW070605120726
47909CB00007B/2446

* 9 7 8 0 6 9 2 9 8 2 2 9 7 *